Blood Moon Rider

Blood Moon Rider

Zack C. Waters

Pineapple Press, Inc.
Sarasota, Florida

Inquiries should be addressed to:

Pineapple Press, Inc.
P.O. Box 3889
Sarasota, Florida 34230
www.pineapplepress.com

Library of Congress Cataloging-in-Publication Data

Waters, Zack C., 1946-
    Blood moon rider / Zack C. Waters. — 1st ed.
        p. cm.
    Summary: After his father's death in World War II, fourteen-year-old Harley Wallace tries to join the Marines but is, instead, sent to live with his grandfather in Peru Landing, Florida, where he soon joins a covert effort to stop Nazis from destroying a secret airbase on Tampa Bay.
    ISBN-13: 978-1-56164-350-9 (hardback : alk. paper)
    ISBN-10: 1-56164-350-5 (hardback : alk. paper)
    [1. Grandfathers—Fiction.   2. Heroes—Fiction.   3. World War, 1939-1945—Fiction.   4. Ranch life—Florida—Fiction.   5. Orphans—Fiction.   6. Florida—History—20th century—Fiction.]   I. Title.
PZ7.W264368Blo 2006
[Fic]—dc22

                                                                2005030749

First Edition
10 9 8 7 6 5 4 3 2 1

Printed in the United States of America

To Vonda,
For her love, patience, and constant encouragement

Proclaim this among the nations:
Prepare for war!
Rouse the warriors!
Let all the fighting men draw near and attack.
Beat your plowshares into swords
And your pruning hooks into spears.
Let the weakling say, "I am strong."
Joel 3:9–10

1

Road Trip

Blame for all my trouble must fall squarely on the shoulders of my stepmother, Rita. In fairness to her, I have never quite decided if she was wicked or just weak. She married my father four years after my real mother died. I believe that Rita really loved my father, but she never seemed to like the lonely life of a Marine officer's wife. One thing is certain though. She always hated me.

Rita went through three bottles of beer before the notification team—a Marine chaplain and a young lieutenant—finished delivering the news that my father had been killed in action.

My father had been a Marine aviator stationed at Wake Island, a tiny, worthless flyspeck of coral and sand located in the Pacific Ocean. After the Japanese destroyed the Pacific fleet at Pearl Harbor and occupied Guam, no one doubted that Wake Island would be their next target.

There were about 450 Marines stationed on Wake, and it is part of the Leatherneck's credo never to surrender a position without a fight. My father took off on the second day of the battle and found himself in the middle of a sky full of Japanese Zeroes. His body washed ashore during the night, and his buddies buried him in an unmarked grave.

Rita really kicked her drinking into high gear as soon as the two officers left our apartment. She took her purse and left, to return fifteen minutes later with three bottles of cheap whiskey. I locked myself in my room and finally cried myself to sleep.

I awoke the next morning to find my stepmother gone. She had packed my bag and left a sealed letter addressed to one Perry Lang Wallace, a Sunshine Bus Lines ticket to Peru Landing, and six dollars in cash, mostly in quarters and dimes. Rita also scrawled a note telling me to go to my grandfather's ranch and she would send for me later. I never heard from Rita again.

I locked the door behind me and hitchhiked down to the Marine recruiter's office. We lived in Beaufort, South Carolina, near the Marines' Parris Island recruit training center. I loved the village's old houses, live oaks draped with Spanish moss, and the omnipresent smell of the sea. That day I hardly noticed them.

A grizzled sergeant sat behind a battered, wooden desk, pouring rum from a brown paper sack into his morning coffee. He glanced at me with one bloodshot eye and then went back to shuffling papers and gulping his brew.

I snapped to attention and barked in my deepest voice, "I'm here to join up."

The sergeant looked me up and down and burst out laughing. "Quit wasting my time," he snorted. "The Corps ain't that hard up yet."

"I want to join the Marines," I repeated, but despite my best effort, my voice cracked a little.

"How old are you, boy. Ten or twelve?"

I resented that guess. I would turn fourteen in two days and thought of myself as almost a man.

"I'm eighteen," I lied.

"Yeah, and I'm the Pope. Where are your mama and papa, boy?"

After a little prodding, I spilled my guts. I told the sergeant about my father, how Rita had disappeared, and my burning desire to kill the Japs.

"I knew your father," he said, sadly shaking his head. "A good man, and a darn good Marine. Wait a few years, Harley Wallace, and you'll make a fine Marine too."

The noncom pulled up a chair for me and dialed the phone. I knew he was talking to someone on the base at Parris Island, but I blocked out the conversation. I stared at posters of Uncle Sam and his courageous Leathernecks. I knew, that if given the chance, I could fight bravely too.

The young Marine chaplain that I had met the previous day came to pick me up. He was rail thin, bald, and had the saddest face I have ever seen. The chaplain talked to me in a kindly way about God's love and not giving in to hatred or despair as he drove me to the bus station. He seemed to be a good man, and meant well, but he may as well have been preaching to a rock. I was angry with God and Rita, filled with self-pity, and brimming over with a murderous rage towards the Japanese. Nothing on earth would stop me from avenging my father, I silently vowed.

There must be a thousand small towns and crossroads between Beaufort, South Carolina, and Peru Landing, Florida. I started counting the number of times the bus stopped, but fell asleep sometime after we crossed the Georgia state line.

At almost every stop, poor Southern families kept reenacting the same scene. A boy, eighteen or nineteen years old, would be standing by the side of the road, clutching a battered suitcase, tow sack, or grocery bag, solemnly shaking hands with his father while his mother stood off to the side crying. He was going off to be a soldier. A couple of times the young man looked older, wearing overalls, and holding tightly to a frightened young woman while a baby bawled in the dirt near their feet. I couldn't help wondering how many of these young men would return to their families and their hardscrabble farms.

My real troubles began shortly after the bus crossed over into Florida. There is a saying that "no good deed goes unpunished," and I soon learned the truth of that old saw, in spades.

At a crossroads between Jasper and Live Oak the bus stopped to take on a pregnant woman. Luggage jammed the aisle, and sweaty people occupied all the seats. She was a black lady, so state law required her to stand in the aisle, as close to the back of the bus as she could squeeze. She stood beside me as the bus clattered down the hard road, hanging onto the metal seat frame behind my head. She moaned in pain a time or two when the vehicle hit a bump, but said nothing. The further along we went, the more her legs wobbled. A few minutes of that convinced me that any minute she might topple over and deliver her baby right in my lap.

I knew the rules, having been raised at military bases throughout the South. I just did not care. I rose and gently took her arm and guided her into my seat. She looked frightened for a moment or two and then managed a weak smile of appreciation.

The white lady in the seat next to the window looked up at me, her face a mask of shock and disapproval. You could tell that she was torn between our Southern customs and sympathy for a suffering member of her gender. She finally turned her face to the window and pretended not to notice. Two young white men in the seat behind me swallowed hard a couple of times, but said nothing.

An old woman, with a stringy neck and frizzy white hair, started all the trouble. She perched uncomfortably on an aisle seat right behind the bus driver. I had been watching her since she got on the bus in South Georgia. Anyone could tell by the way she acted that she had a screw loose. She kept jerking her head back every few minutes as if she were afraid that Death would sneak up on her and she could catch him in the act. Maybe just having so many men around terrified her.

When she spotted the pregnant black lady in my seat her eyes flew open wide—first with surprise, and then with rage.

"There's a nigra in the middle section," she yelled, leaning forward. "A *nigra* in the middle section!"

The driver—a chubby fellow with a kindly face and wearing a sweat-stained Sunshine Bus Lines shirt—tried to calm her. He'd been watching the whole thing through his rearview mirror, and he had looked relieved when I seated the pregnant lady. I don't think he relished the idea of delivering a baby on a hot, crowded bus by the side of the road. He said something to the frizzy-haired woman, but she started screeching that she would report him to the district office. I could tell that he was wasting his breath.

In the end, bus rules and Southern tradition won out over simple common sense. He pulled the bus over to the side of the highway but left the engine running. Dodging the feet and baggage blocking the aisle, the driver stumbled back to where we sat and whispered something to the pregnant lady. With a look of resignation, she pulled herself up and resumed her position, clinging to the seat frame for support.

He looked over at me, and said, "You come with me. I want to keep an eye on you." He grabbed me by the shirt and dragged me to the front of the bus. He sent a tall young man, wearing a suit three sizes too small, back to my seat, and sat me down in the seat behind the frizzy-haired woman.

"Now you behave," he said, and went back to his seat.

The frizzy-haired crone turned around and glared at me until the bus had gone a good two miles. I just sat there with a stupid grin on my face until she turned back around, mumbling something about "nigra-loving simpletons." I wished I had a hammer, but since none was handy, I just slumped back in my seat and prayed for some other form of revenge.

Preachers will tell you that God works in mysterious

ways, but this time He outdid Himself.

The driver had placed me on a bench beside a middle-aged fat man, who had slept through the entire little melodrama. A brown paper bag rested on his lap, containing the half-eaten remains of a meatloaf sandwich and some cookie crumbs. Several of the big Florida Charley roaches were busily harvesting the remains of the sleeping man's lunch. I reached over to grab one. I intended to drop the creature on old frizzy hair's lap as I got off the bus. Unfortunately, I missed my target, and the roach took wing, flying right down the neck of the old hag's blouse.

Well, you have never seen such an uproar. The old woman came unglued. She hopped to her feet like she had been jabbed with a hot poker. She screamed, she yelled, she flopped around and fell over a suitcase, falling face first on the floor. The battered piece of luggage popped open, and the frizzy-haired woman jumped up from the wreckage, with a pair of men's drawers on her hands. Forgetting where she was, she began clawing buttons from her blouse, slapping at the roach, which had apparently headed south toward her girdle.

A slack-jawed hick, sitting in the middle seats, laughed so hard he looked like he was about to burst a blood vessel. Turning to his seatmate, he yelled in a voice loud enough to be heard throughout the bus, "This beats that hoochie-koochie show we saw in Jacksonville!"

The whole bus erupted in laughter. Caught up in the fun, I slapped my knee and laughed so hard I lost track of old frizzy hair. That was a serious mistake.

The enraged hag had now forgotten about that Charley roach, but she had not forgotten about me. She came at my throat with those hawklike talons. I spotted her out of the corner of my eye and dodged to one side. She slammed past me and hit the sleeping fat man. He snapped awake to find a pair of underwear on his face and a crazed woman clawing at his eyes. Only half-awake, and confused by the noise and excitement, the fat man must have thought his wife had attacked him. He threw his arms over his face for protection and scrunched up against the bus window screeching, "My heavens Harriet, I ain't been messing with no other women!" The men on the bus again roared with laughter.

Old frizzy-hair had by now set her sights on me again, and she would probably have killed me if it had not been for the bus driver. He managed to pull the bus to the shoulder of the road and jumped between the old crone and me. "Get back in your seat," he yelled at the woman, pushing her. "And for God's sake, cover yourself up, lady."

Suddenly realizing that she was in a bus filled with leering men with an open blouse, she bent over in her seat, fumbled with her buttons, and wailed like she had been slapped.

The driver grabbed me and my satchel, opened the door, and threw us both down by the side of the road. Pointing down the blacktop, he shouted, "Pentecost is a mile and a half down the road. You can catch another bus there. You ain't going no further with me!"

Before I could utter a word of protest, the bus doors slammed shut and I could hear the harried driver grinding gears to get the coach started. I was so mad I couldn't see straight. I looked around, and since there is not a decent rock in that part of Florida, I grabbed a handful of clay clumps. I ran along the side of the departing bus, pelting the frizzy-haired woman's window with dirt clods until I could no longer keep up.

2

Adventures in Petty Theft

I stood in the dust by the side of the road feeling totally dejected and alone. Despite what the driver had said, I knew that the Sunshine Bus Lines people would never give me a second ticket. The driver's report of the incident would label me a troublemaker. With the buses full of men going to join the armed services and me with no important relatives in the area, Sunshine could afford to ignore my demands for passage to Peru Landing. I had to face the facts. I was alone and friendless.

From a big map I'd studied in the Macon bus terminal, I knew that Peru Landing is located near the center of the Wildcat Bay region on the Gulf of Mexico. (Wildcat Bay stretches south from where the peninsula juts away from the panhandle like the half-opened blade of a jackknife.) I reckoned my destination still lay about a hundred miles to the southwest. But I figured that when I found the right road, I could get most of the way to my grandfather's ranch hitching rides with farmers and traveling salesmen. The rest of the way I would just have to walk.

I decided to avoid town and headed south along a packed clay road. Most of the roads in Florida consisted of either packed clay or a pair of ruts worn through the sand and wiregrass by the weight of wagons and trucks. The state had managed to pave only a few of the main roads. The local people called these tire-destroying mixtures of tar and little granite stones "hard roads." I knew that when I got south of Pentecost, I could just find a paved road heading southwest and start thumbing.

A few widely scattered houses lined the road I chose. I hadn't gone far when the wonderful smell of something baking stopped me dead in my tracks. I had last eaten at the Macon bus stop, spending twenty cents of my six-dollar stake on a handful of soda crackers, a wedge of dry, tasteless cheese, a candy bar, and a grape Nehi soft drink. That had been several hours before, and the smell of that pie caused my stomach to start growling and rumbling.

Slipping off the road, I followed my nose. Picking my way through the thickets, it didn't take me long to discover the source of that delicious scent. The odor came from a modern brick house, not very large or fancy, but neat and well kept. Around back, I spotted a cobbler sitting in the kitchen window, cooling. I took a quick look around. There seemed to be miles of woods stretching out in all directions behind the house. Enough leaves clung to the trees and bushes, even in January, to hide a lone boy and his pie.

Stealing that pastry was the easiest thing I have ever done. First, I checked to make certain that the homeowner did not have a dog in the yard. Seeing none, I hopped that little waist-high picket fence, scampered up under the kitchen window, grabbed the pie, and ran like I had bloodhounds nipping at my heels.

The gods of larceny seemed to be smiling upon me because just before I snatched the pastry, I heard a telephone ringing in the house. I figured I had at least ten or fifteen minutes to get away while the lady of the house gossiped with a neighbor. The entire theft took less than thirty seconds.

I scampered through the woods for about two minutes before dropping down with my back to a big live oak tree. I dipped my fingers into the hot goo and started stuffing it into my mouth. The cobbler tasted great, and within five minutes

I had wolfed it all down. I leaned back against that oak for a minute to savor the warm feel of a full belly and a successful venture into the world of petty theft.

"You ain't having a very good day, are you kid?" a rough voice drawled.

I jumped up, planning to dash off into the woods. The voice, now icy cold, stopped me dead in my tracks.

"Don't do it kid! Don't make me shoot you in the leg."

I turned around slowly. The man stood there, whip thin, sad-eyed, with a droopy handlebar mustache, leaning heavily on a cane. Pinned to his shirt was a badge. It read: "Bullock County Sheriff." In his hand he carried a pistol, cocked and ready to fire. It read: "Smith and Wesson."

The whole situation suddenly seemed so stupid.

"Someone called the police over a pie?" I asked in disbelief.

"I said you ain't having a real lucky day. You should not have stolen my pie." He laughed, but the sound revealed little hint of good humor. "My wife cooked it for our anniversary supper."

He handcuffed me and took me to his house. His wife stood in the kitchen door, obviously concerned. She was a plump lady, about the lawman's age, dressed in a simple cotton dress and an apron. She wore glasses. A happy smile of relief played across her face when she saw her hero returning with the dangerous criminal in tow.

The sheriff became a completely different person around her. He obviously adored her and could not look at her without smiling like a lovesick puppy. It was disgusting.

While Anne McCully, as she introduced herself, peeled more apples and talked to me about the secrets for making a great pie, the sheriff went through my valise. When he got to the sealed letter Rita had written, he looked at me and said, "Perry Lang Wallace?"

"He's my grandfather," I replied.

"He know you're coming for a visit?"

"I don't think so," I replied. Which was true. I doubted that Rita had had the nerve to call him, and I knew that the Marines would stop with notification of next of kin. They would naturally assume that Rita would contact the rest of the family.

"Maybe you better tell me your story," he said.

So I told him and his wife about how my father had been killed at Wake Island, how my stepmother had left me, why the driver had thrown me off the bus, how I started walking to Peru Landing, and finally, how I had snitched the pie. I threw in a couple of times how I had been dizzy with hunger at the time I gave into temptation, and even tried to sound contrite about stealing their pie.

Mrs. McCully cried softly when I finished, but I could tell that I had failed to convince the sheriff of my innocence. It's funny how that works. Boys lie, but I could usually convince my women teachers in Beaufort if I made my lips quiver like I was about to cry. Old Mr. Owens, my only male teacher, would not believe me if I said the sun set in the west.

Sheriff McCully gave me that sarcastic smile again. "Well, I guess I was more right than I knew about you having a run of bad luck. My neighbor made a telephone call to warn me that he had seen a young hooligan skulking around my back yard." He laughed at the irony of the situation, but I felt pretty steamed at his enjoyment of my misery.

To show how little he trusted me, he cuffed me to his refrigerator door. I found his lack of faith so disturbing that I tested the weight of the appliance a couple of times to see if I could move it. It was a useless gesture. I would have had three hernias before I even got it to the kitchen door.

Sheriff McCully and his wife spent a long time in their living room. I could hear them mumbling, but could not make

out what they said. The sheriff turned the crank of the telephone a couple of times, but I had no idea whom he called or why.

Anne McCully came back in the kitchen while her husband made his calls. She did not share what they said, but she smiled and winked at me as she began putting the finishing touches on supper. That relieved my mind somewhat. Her friendly manner seemed designed to assure me that whatever happened, I had a friend in my corner.

I celebrated the couple's anniversary meal with them. I felt certain it was Mrs. McCully's idea. I had not noticed any pictures of children in any part of the house I had seen, and I wondered if Anne had found a way to enjoy what nature had denied her—if only for a little while.

I dug into that supper of roast beef, mashed potatoes, cooked carrots, green beans, corn bread, and sweet tea with gusto. I even forced myself to down a healthy wedge of apple pie, just to be polite.

As I finished dessert, a deputy arrived. He was an old man, unshaven and wearing that same hangdog, defeated look I had seen when sharecroppers came to town. He wore overalls, with his star pinned to the bib.

Anne McCully kissed my cheek and whispered for me not to worry, and then the deputy put me in the back of a battered, black Ford. Some semi-literate flunky had stenciled the words "Bulloc County Sherif" on the side of the car in blue paint.

The deputy said nothing to me during the trip to the jail. He spent the time busily working on a huge cud of chewing tobacco and dripping the juices in a coffee cup that rested on the seat between his legs. Several of my father's old Marine buddies chewed tobacco, but they swallowed the juices. I have never seen anything as disgusting as the old lawman's dip-chew-spit routine.

We parked at the back of the courthouse in front of a heavy steel door. The silent deputy knocked on the door with the butt of his shotgun. Almost immediately, a portal flew open, and a hard-looking man with close-cropped hair stared at us for a second. He didn't speak, but soon the jail door swung open to let us in. The gatekeeper looked a lot like a bull—squat, heavy, and muscular. He didn't even wait for us to enter before he retreated to a small wire cage where he had a cup of steaming coffee and a Western novel.

A narrow walkway led to the second floor, which housed the sheriff's office and the cellblock. I lugged my satchel up the steep stairs until the silent deputy and I reached the landing. The sheriff's office faced the stairs, and a heavy wooden desk sat in front of the doors. During the workday, a deputy would have been on duty to screen the sheriff's visitors and check people visiting prisoners for weapons.

To the left was a row of eight cells. Bright lights shown down the hallway of the cellblock, and I could see and hear the prisoners. Two were obviously drunks. One man crouched on his hands and knees retching into a slop jar. The other tunelessly mumbled the words to a church song.

The third prisoner was a skinny black youth, not much older than me. He wore tattered pants and a work shirt. His face, arms, and feet were badly scratched as though he had been dragged through a briar patch. He stared straight ahead with blank, defeated eyes.

The silent deputy saw me looking at the young prisoner.

"Chicken thief," he said by way of explanation, and spat at a cuspidor leaning against the cellblock door. Part of the brown glob missed the brass jug and splattered down the hallway between the cells. None of the prisoners seemed to notice.

I dreaded spending the night in one of those cells. The bright lights would shine in my eyes, and the smell strangled me, even from the landing. The barred rooms seemed cold and alien. The cells had no mattresses, with only a single, thin blanket serving as a bed.

The deputy motioned me to follow him, and we turned to the right.

Behind a closed door, opposite the cellblock, was a single jail cell. It contained a toilet, a decent mattress, and a thick pane of glass over the barred window. The deputy unlocked the cell door and motioned me inside.

I must have looked surprised.

"Female cell," the deputy muttered. "Mrs. McCully said to make sure you were comfortable."

So much talking seemed to exhaust him, and he shut the door without another sound. He left the door to my cell open, but he locked the outside door. I guessed that the lawman trusted me, but only up to a point.

I stretched out on the cot and took off my shoes. The long, hard day had completely worn me out, but I still had trouble falling asleep. A smattering of rain beaded the glass windowpane. It would be cold in the morning.

When I finally drifted off to sleep, I rolled and tossed all night, haunted by strange and terrifying nightmares. In my vision, a demon with the same lifeless eyes as the young chicken thief chased me through a dungeon, while my father, his Marine uniform wildly flaming, tumbled endlessly toward a cold, black sea.

3

Second Chances

Sheriff McCully arrived around 7:30 and brought me breakfast. The plate held generous portions of scrambled eggs (still
warm), crisp bacon, biscuits, and cane syrup. I ate like a man
facing a firing squad. I still believe that Anne McCully is one of
the finest people I ever met, and the best cook.

About an hour later, an older man came trudging up the
stairs. The first thing I noticed about him was the scars. The right
side of his face looked like it had been gouged and scored by a
drunken engraver. He had no cheekbone on that side of his face.
His thick, white hair drooped to the collar of his coat and framed
his deeply tanned face. He wore a badly wrinkled suit that
smelled faintly of mothballs. He carried a wide-brimmed, floppy
hat in his hands.

I knew immediately that this was my grandfather. He looked
exactly like an older, badly scarred version of my father.

Sheriff McCully came toward him with his hand
outstretched and a smile—a real smile—on his face.

"Well, Perry," he said, warmly shaking hands with the old
man. "I guess I found a way to get you to come for a visit. All I had
to do is arrest your grandson."

"That'll do it every time," my grandfather replied. The retort may have been intended as masculine banter, but coming from the sad and troubled old man, it sounded creepy rather than good-natured.

My grandfather looked me up and down, coolly measuring me the way a scientist might examine his specimen.

I had only seen Grandfather Wallace once in my life when we took my real mother back to Peru Landing for burial when I was just a kid of five. I don't remember much about that visit except how desolate my father had been and that I cried the whole time we were in Florida.

My father almost never talked about Grandfather Wallace. I remember only once that he said anything positive about the old man. I had been worried after my mother died, afraid that dad would die too, killed fighting in a war. Father reminded me that the Wallace clan had always been a race of warriors, spinning tales of Scotland and ancestors who fought the English (both in the old country and America), Indians, and Yankees. He told me how grandfather had a cigar box full of medals from the Great War, that somebody named Marshal Foch gave him something called the *Croix de Guerre* and kissed him on the cheeks. Anyway, my dad once told me it is better to die fighting for what is right than to live a thousand years as a coward and that he learned that from his dad. I looked at this old man and wondered if this could be that brave medal-winner.

Sheriff McCully apparently felt the tension. "Why don't we go into my office," he suggested, "and get to the bottom of things."

At the sheriff's urging, I gave Grandfather Wallace the letter from Rita, and we waited silently while he read it. After a few moments he got up, the papers dangling carelessly in his long fingers, and stared out at the cold and wind-swept streets. After a few minutes he turned back around and sat heavily in his chair. "Stupid, stupid, oh God, how stupid," he moaned, and then stared at the ceiling.

With the sheriff's prodding, I told again the story of my trip to Pentecost. The old man gave no indication that he heard me or cared about my odyssey.

"Harley Wallace," the sheriff said when I concluded my tale. "I guess I had better get used to that name."

I looked at him, surprised. I had just assumed that he would release me into the custody of my grandfather. Now I wondered if he intended to hold me over for trial.

He laughed at the look on my face. "Aunt Ruth Ella Hogebaum is a fine old black lady who lives south of Pentecost," he explained. "Last night she came by the house and wanted to know if I could find the name of the young gentleman who caused the ruckus on the bus yesterday. Seems her daughter Sara gave birth to a strapping baby boy yesterday afternoon. Sara wants to name the baby for the white boy who helped her on the bus." He laughed at the irony of the situation. "Harley Wallace Raulerson. Kinda rolls off the tongue, don't it."

We stayed in the office for about twenty more minutes. Sheriff McCully did most of the talking. He had, McCully explained, been pretending not to know my grandfather when he handcuffed me to the refrigerator, but they had once been friends. He'd called the sheriff in Timucua County and asked the lawman to get word to Perry Wallace that his grandson was in custody in Pentecost.

My grandfather said little during this time. Most of his responses to direct questions were grunts or single-syllable words.

After a while, Grandfather Wallace got up and said he needed to find gasoline for the trip back to Peru Landing. McCully gave directions to a nearby gas station, and we watched as the old man shuffled down the staircase. I didn't know if he meant to take me with him. I wasn't sure which would be worse—going with him or . . . well, I didn't know where else I could go.

The sheriff motioned for me to come over to him. We stood by the window and watched as my grandfather got into a battered old Ford truck. A hound dog, which had been sleeping on the front seat, greeted the old man, putting its paws on its master's chest and licking his scarred face.

"You don't know much about Perry Wallace, do you?" the sheriff asked.

I shook my head.

"Well, I do. He's a legend in these parts, you know?"

Again I shook my head.

"He owns one of the largest cattle ranches in the state. Most people think he has lived like a hermit for almost twenty years—since your grandmother died. He loved her so much, it seems like a part of him died with her."

I said nothing.

"He's a good man. The kind of man you want with you in a fight."

I offered no encouragement for him to continue, but he seemed determined for me to hear him out.

"He won all kinds of medals during the Great War. Led a twenty-man squad of Marines into some little village in France. A regiment of Germans attacked the place, but Perry had orders to hold his position at all hazards. Well, you know the Leathernecks and their orders. They held that God-forsaken hamlet until reinforcements finally arrived. Only four men came back alive, and they were shot all to pieces."

"Is that where he got the scars on his face?" I asked, interested in spite of myself.

"No. He got those scars the same place I got this bum knee. In a shootout with the Tuttle Gang. You know about them?"

"No."

He began rummaging through his desk and telling his story at the same time.

"Well, a couple of years after Perry came back from France, the governor appointed your grandfather sheriff of Timucua County, to finish the term of Sheriff Rawlings."

He pulled out a faded picture of six men and two women. Each of them held a Tommy gun or a shotgun, even the females. They stared at the camera, their youthful faces showing neither remorse nor fear. Some leaned casually against a big Chrysler touring car, as carefree as a church group at a county fair.

"That's them," the sheriff said, tapping the photo with his finger. "They had been raising Cain, robbing banks and stores, all over the Wildcat Bay area for five years. They decided to branch out, and robbed a bank in Tallahassee. That was a big mistake. The father-in-law of the Leon County sheriff owned the bank they robbed, and the sheriff acted like they had stolen his own money. He got five cars full of deputies on the trail of the Tuttles. One of the deputies told me later that the sheriff told them not to come back without the Tuttles and his father-in-law's money."

I tried to imagine the chase scene from the motion pictures I had seen. I could almost hear the whine of the engines and the squeal of tires. I wondered if one of the lawmen balanced on the running board, clinging for dear life to the window posts while trying to get a shot at the fleeing bandits.

"Coley Turner, the Bullock County sheriff at the time, determined to set up a roadblock out on Route Seventeen. I was a rookie cop at the time. Ol' Coley called Perry Wallace for help, and he brought two deputies with him.

"Well, sir, about three o'clock in the morning the Tuttle Gang rolled up to that barricade. They tried to run through the cars and trucks blocking the highway, but we shot out the tires. They had Tommy guns and had been drinking pretty heavily. Anyway, they came out of that shot-up Chrysler firing away. The Tuttles were bad people, and had sworn never to be taken alive."

I had seen that scene in a lot of gangster movies. The bold robbers shooting their way out of a police trap. I pictured streaks of light cutting through the black night and could almost hear echoes of Jimmy Cagney's insane laughter.

"Sheriff Turner went down in the first volley," the sheriff continued, "shot in the head and chest. Two of the other deputies died fighting. I took a stray bullet in the knee and slumped down beside my automobile. My leg hurt like fury, but I kept on shooting. The members of the gang who were still alive headed toward my car while I was trying to reload. I figured I was as good as dead.

"Just then, Perry Wallace jumped up from behind the trunk of the Timucua County car. He was bleeding like a stuck pig, but he had that old Springfield rifle he'd carried during the war. He had the Tuttles right where he wanted them—with their hands full of moneybags and out in the open. He just slaughtered them. I have never seen faster, or more accurate, shooting. Old Billy Tuttle, the leader of the gang, went down first with a shot in the head. Perry killed two of the outlaws within ten feet of me."

I tried to picture the tired old man I had just met as a mighty warrior. It just did not add up.

"We held the two survivors, a man and a woman, in a ditch until the Tallahassee police arrived. Every newspaper in the South carried accounts of the gun battle. They had pictures of your grandfather and me on the front pages for weeks. Perry Wallace could have run for governor that year and been elected."

He shook his head sadly, recalling the fall of a giant.

"Then everything changed. The doctors diagnosed your

grandmother with cancer. When she died, a lot of people assumed that Perry began living like a hermit, but I know he has a lot of friends in Timucua County. He just avoided any publicity and started staying pretty close to his ranch.

"As soon as your father, Davey, got old enough, he ran off and joined the Marines. I don't know what happened between Perry and your father, but I take it they weren't close."

I nodded. The sheriff should have received an award for the understatement of the year. In truth, I was kind of frightened. If I was going to live with my grandfather, I had no idea what my life there would be like, but I guessed it would be neither easy nor pleasant. I tried to formulate a plan. If the old man turned out to be too awful, what could I do? Run away? Try to find Rita? I wondered if Mrs. McCully might take me in if I showed up at her door one cold night.

"You afraid?" the sheriff asked, as if he were reading my mind.

I didn't know what to say. The thought of the future scared me, but no fourteen-year-old kid wants an adult knowing a thing like that. I just shrugged my shoulders.

"I didn't mean to embarrass you," McCully said with a tired smile. "I was just hoping. You see, I think my friend Perry Wallace needs a second chance. You may be the one to give it to him."

Just then my grandfather returned, and the sheriff never got a chance to finish what he had on his mind. After hurried goodbyes, we headed back downstairs. I noticed that the two drunks were sleeping it off, but the boy with the dead eyes was not in his cell.

I stopped and turned to Sheriff McCully. "Where is he?" I asked. "The young chicken thief."

"I told you I believe in second chances," he said, and winked at me.

My grandfather and I got into the truck and headed south

out of Pentecost. The old hound sat with his head on his master's shoulder. I stroked his head and neck, and his tail wagged appreciatively against my side.

"His name is Red," the old man said.

I wondered why the old man named a black and white dog Red. I thought it might be a joke, but Grandfather explained after a long pause. "Used to be Red Pepper, but it got shortened over time. I guess we've both lost some fire through the years."

The dog cocked his head for a moment at hearing his name, but soon stretched out and went to sleep. He laid his head in my grandfather's lap and rested his hindquarters in my lap. We rode for a long time in silence.

Out the window of the truck, the bleak countryside seemed to shiver in the short Florida winter. The leaves still clung to the branches of the trees and the Spanish moss quivered in the breeze like an old man's beard. There were few houses once we left Pentecost, only mile upon mile of pine and oak shuddering in the chilly wind along bayous and flat prairies. Here and there a cabbage palm or the white trunk of a sycamore tree broke the monotony. A smattering of rain fell, off and on, and the dark gray clouds hung just above the treetops.

At Garfish Creek, the old man pulled the truck off the side of the road. The hound jumped out of the truck to explore the nearby woods, marking trees and bushes with his scent. We leaned against the side of the old Ford, watching Red's antics.

"Your dad and I used to fish this river," my grandfather said suddenly. "Before things got bad between us. We'd put in here and float all the way down to Yancy. We'd camp the night at Ulster Hill and cook our fish and talk."

"My father loved to fish," I said, not knowing how else to respond.

"Are you angry?" he asked out of the blue.

I nodded.

"Me too," he said, in a sharp, bitter tone.

"You mad at me?" I queried.

"Oh, no," he said quickly. "Don't you ever think that! No, I'm mad at the Japs. I'm mad at the government for sticking a few Marines on a rock in the middle of nowhere and leaving them hanging out to dry. God forgive me, but I'm mad at Him for taking my son away. I'm furious with Rita for abandoning my grandson and not having the courage to tell me about Davey's death except in that ranting letter of a drunk. But mostly, I'm mad at myself."

"You?" I asked. "Why?"

"Because I was a lousy father. I never told Davey how much I loved him and how proud I was of him. I never tried to tell him why I stopped talking to him. I saw so much of his mother in him that, when she died, it was like a knife in my heart every time I looked at him."

I had no idea what to say, so I didn't say anything.

"Did my son ever say much about me?" he asked after a long silence.

"He loved you," I said. I suppose it was lie. I didn't tell him how a dark shadow passed over my father's face whenever someone made the mistake of mentioning Grandfather Wallace's name.

"Did he really?" Grandfather wondered, the doubt obvious in his voice.

I nodded again, and we were both quiet for a long time. Finally, he stood and whistled for Red.

"I made a lot of mistakes with Davey," he said, his voice cracking with emotion. "But I promise, Harley, that I won't repeat those mistakes with you. I will try to be the father to you that I should have been to Davey, but wasn't."

4

Introductions, Past and Present

We reached the Wildcat River shortly after noon. The Wildcat splits Timucua County in half. The river's source is a small spring in the piney woods of Union County. From there, it meanders through the rich farmland and forests of central Florida, in some places little more than a creek. A few miles east of Yancy, the river begins to widen and turns back upon itself, to begin its final sprint to the Gulf of Mexico. The water there is boisterous and stained dark brown by the tannic acid from the large groves of oak trees that grow along its banks. The Wildcat is almost a quarter of a mile wide when it empties into the Gulf at Peru Landing.

Grandfather told me all about the Timucua County land-marks as we rolled southwest. Once Grandfather started talking, it was hard to get him to stop. I knew he was desperately trying to make amends for the quiet treatment my father had been subjected to, but I admit I liked it better than the gloomy silence I had endured during the first part of the journey.

I soon discovered that questions never received a "yes" or "no" answer. Answers circled in spirals, like a hawk searching for rabbits, and somewhere before it ended would be the answer to your question—and so much more. The answers generally included some local history, a cast of colorful characters, opinion, and the unwritten knowledge of several generations.

When we reached the bridge at Dingle's Ferry, Grandfather turned the old truck to the west.

"I thought we'd run into the Landing before we go home," he said. "I got some things to take care of. Besides, we need to get you some decent work clothes."

We passed a battered sign that used to announce, "Peru Landing, 12 miles." Someone had perforated it with buckshot. To add to that indignity, some anonymous wit had changed the "r" into an "e," and blotted out the "u," using bright orange house paint. The sign, riddled with holes, now read, "Pee Landing, 12 miles." In spite of myself, I laughed at this sad warning.

"You have a dangerous sense of humor, Harley," my grandfather grumbled. He didn't fool me. I could see the corners of his mouth turned up as he tried to repress a smile.

To change the subject, I asked, "How did Peru Landing get its name?"

"Well, according to what my grandfather told me, here's the story. Mordecai Cohen was the first white settler in this area. He established a trading post on a series of high hills along the north bank of the Wildcat, where it empties into the Gulf of Mexico."

The answer lasted all the way to town. Boiled down to its essentials, Mr. Mordecai Cohen, the first white settler in Timucua County, had read everything he could get his hands on about the exploration of South America. He loved the wood engravings in the magazines showing the mountains of Peru and named the low hills near the mouth of the Wildcat for that country.

"Now the highest hill I have ever seen in Florida misses the heights of the Andes Mountains by several thousand feet," Grandfather concluded with a smirk, "but he named his trading post Peru Landing. The name stuck, and it's been that ever since."

My grandfather was a terrific storyteller and seemed to know something about every subject. I listened enthralled by the web of history and folklore the old man spun. I also felt a nagging sadness. I thought of the long years of silence my father endured, while my grandfather could have done so much to lessen their mutual loneliness. I wondered if my father had ever heard the story of how Peru Landing got its name. I doubted it.

When we finally pulled up in front of the Peru Landing General Mercantile, Grandfather opened the door to let Red out, but the old man made no effort to get out. After a while he said, "I'd like to have a memorial service for Davey—if you don't mind."

I hated the idea of sharing possession of my father's memory with anyone. I had nothing else left of my father except the certainty that he dearly loved me. Still, my grandfather obviously felt the need to do something public to honor my father, and if it made him feel better, why should I throw cold water on his dream?

"I guess it's okay," I mumbled.

We sat for a few minutes, not talking. A two-block area of brick and stucco shops and houses lined the main street of Peru Landing. This downtown area had once been the pride of the booming little city, but most of the buildings now sat empty and forlorn. The windows of the abandoned buildings were either broken or boarded up. Even the Broken Spur Saloon, which at the turn of the twentieth century had been one of the most famous cattlemen's watering holes in west Florida, crouched along the main street, deserted and decaying. A real estate agent had nailed a big "For Sale" sign to the door, but I doubted it would ever sell. The cattle pens, rooted in the marshy plain beside the blue green waters of the Gulf, littered the flats like tombstones of a bygone era of prosperity. Peru Landing had one foot already in the grave and the other on a banana peel.

Peru Landing General Mercantile offered a stark contrast to the rest of the town. It gave off an aura of comfortable prosperity. Several old cowmen lounged on the benches in front of the store, whittling, chewing, and telling old-man stories. They all hollered greetings to Grandfather Wallace as we entered the store.

Electric lights lit up the entire showroom, and the shelves were stocked with every conceivable type of merchandise. It surprised me to see the latest fashions for women hanging in orderly rows beside the unchanging work garb preferred by men who spend their lives outdoors. Food, tools, saddles, auto parts, radios, and furniture filled almost every square foot of the Mercantile.

Martin Levy greeted my grandfather with a happy smile. It's hard to imagine two friends more different in appearance. Mr. Levy towered over my wiry grandfather by several inches, and the storekeeper was getting a little thick around the middle. Mr. Levy wore a starched white shirt and a little gray bow tie that matched the color of his trousers. Someone told me once to never trust a man who sported a bow tie, but the merchant had a genial manner that put everyone entering the store at ease. Grandfather obviously liked and trusted the storekeeper. That was all I needed to know, for now.

Grandfather Wallace introduced me as "Davey's son," and Mr. Levy shook my hand. After telling the storekeeper about the death of my father, he said, "I need to make some arrangements."

Mr. Levy told me to grab a soft drink and a candy bar, and the two men retreated into a little office.

I rummaged through the icy water of the big, red Coca Cola box until I located an orange Nehi. I finally decided on a Clark bar for my treat, and I ate it while I wandered down aisle after aisle, marveling at the vast array of products the store offered.

After a few minutes, Grandfather and Mr. Levy came out of the office. The storekeeper had prepared a list that he kept rechecking to make sure that they had not forgotten something important.

"I hope that you and Leah and young Judah can come to the memorial on Monday," Grandfather said.

"Leah and I will be there, but Judah has run off to join the service."

"Well, my hands Henry and Willie and Dilby joined the Navy as soon as they heard about Pearl Harbor. I don't see how I can run my ranch without some young cowmen, but most of the big spreads are short of hands to work their cows. Seems like all of our young men just can't wait to join up and fight."

After a moment, Mr. Levy asked, "Who you gonna get to conduct the services?"

"I thought I would get Brother Stumpy, if he hasn't run off to join the Marines. By the way, do you suppose you have some work clothes that will fit Harley?"

Martin Levy looked at me carefully, and then went and pulled three pair of thick cotton work pants off the shelf and three light-colored, long sleeve shirts. They fit perfectly.

"Does he need underwear, boots, or a saddle?"

"I guess whatever skivvies he's got will do, and I thought I would give him Davey's old saddle, but I bet he doesn't have any decent boots. Also, with an extra mouth to feed, you probably need to give me some flour, corn meal, canned vegetables, and canned peaches."

We loaded the goods into the back of the truck, whistled for Red, and headed out toward the north along a dirt track that ran parallel to the Gulf.

"I'm going to see Bobby Tate," the old man said. "I need to tell you how he looks before we get to his place. He was shot up pretty badly over in France and breathed in some type of poison gas. I don't want you to be afraid or sick. He's pretty scary looking when you first see him. The government hasn't seen fit to give him a pension, and I try to give him odd jobs when I can."

We pulled up in front of a rickety hut that sat in a grove of palms about a hundred yards from the Gulf. Grandfather honked the horn, and we waited until the door opened before getting out.

I have never seen a more horribly disfigured human than Bobby Tate, before or since that afternoon. He must have once been tall, but now he stooped so badly that I loomed over the battered veteran. He looked as gaunt as a skeleton. His chin had been shot away and he wore a leather pouch, like the pocket of a baseball glove, to cover the area beneath his lower teeth. Every few minutes he hacked, and his whole body contorted in the effort, his emaciated chest heaving as if he were trying to cough up a lung.

Despite his looks, what must have passed for a smile flitted across his face, and a deep baritone voice called, "Well, Lieutenant Wallace, come on in and set a spell."

"Captain Tate, so good to see you."

Suddenly the cab of the truck began to shake like a volcano beginning to erupt. Seeing Bobby Tate, Red had gone crazy in the truck. Grandfather had left his window rolled up, and the old hound bounced around the interior of the cab, yowling, scratching at the windows, and banging his head against the windshield glass until I ran back and threw open the door. Finally free, the dog ran toward the crippled man, bouncing and skipping for joy like a young puppy. Red wagged his tail and leaned gently against the wounded man's leg, as if the animal feared that his full weight would topple the frail human scarecrow. Bobby Tate idly ran his long fingers over the ears of the old hound and made strange cooing sounds through his ghastly mouth.

We went into the hut, and I've never seen so much beauty and so much horror in one place. Paintings in watercolor and oils hung from the walls and lay in orderly stacks in the corners of the room. Pictures of white egrets preening in the sunrise hung next to battle scenes so vivid you could almost smell the fear and cordite. An easel stood in the middle of the room, and a magnificent seascape, almost finished, sat waiting for the artist's final brushstrokes.

Grandfather Wallace got right down to business.

"Is the *Mademoiselle* still seaworthy?" he asked.

"She hasn't sent me to the bottom yet," Captain Bobby replied, with that facial movement I took as a smile. "You planning to start running rum up from the Bahamas?"

"No. A little shorter trip. If you feel like it, I would appreciate you running up to Bear Paw Island and delivering a message to my sister and the Manigaults." (He pronounced the name of the famous French Huguenot family as "manny – go.")

"No problem," he said.

"I need you to go today, if possible. My son Davey was killed on Wake Island, and we're having a memorial service at the ranch on Monday. I would be honored if you would come to the service too."

The old soldier shook his head. This news of war and death seemed to unleash a swarm of demons inside his head, and a haunted look replaced his earlier feeble attempts at levity.

Bobby Tate began picking up items from his orderly studio and putting them in a duffel bag. He handed me his army canteen and pointed out the door. "There's a spring about a hundred yards to the east near a big oak tree. Would you mind filling this for me?"

When I got back to the cabin, Grandfather had finished his note to his sister, and we helped Captain Bobby carry his gear to a sleek little sloop. The crippled man was surprisingly agile. He pushed the vessel into the chilly surf, hopped aboard, and began raising the sail without a backward glance.

Grandfather Wallace slipped back into the artist's studio-home and put a ten-dollar bill on the table. Then we got in the truck and headed south through Peru Landing and turned northeast toward cattle country.

"We got one more stop before we head home," the old man said.

"Where?" I asked.

"I wanted to get Brother Stumpy to conduct the service. He works on Loretta Rawling's ranch, and I need to let her know about Davey too."

The Rawlings ranch was about thirty miles inland from the Gulf. Once we left the coast, miles of dark hardwood forests and acres of rich pasture lands stretched out as far as the eye could see.

We stopped once to watch a bear trying to steal the bud out of the top of a cabbage palm. These trees stood like lone sentinels in the open pastures. The branchless trunks rose straight from the ground ten or fifteen feet high and were topped by a wild clump of palm fronds. The bud grew at the top and resembled a small cabbage. Bears loved them more than honey or fresh fish. We sat in silence watching the animal balancing in the limber fronds, and flailing its paws at the treetop like a hairy windmill.

"I've seen them grab ahold of a cabbage and fall over backwards out of the tree. When they recover from the fall, they eat the cabbage on the spot and then go wandering off looking for another," my grandfather explained. "I guess the bears are like men and war. No matter how much it hurts, they like it so much they go looking for another as soon as they're finished with the last one."

I didn't appreciate the old man's sentiments. I thought at the time he had lost his senses. Was this the speech of a warrior feared on two continents? I shook my head.

Grandfather's comment made me wonder about my original impressions of the old man. From the little I had heard about him, I thought he would be a tight-lipped, bitter veteran, despised or feared by the entire region. I found instead a man with many friends who seemed to be both respected and well liked. While he could never be described as loquacious, he certainly seemed to be trying very hard to put me at ease and make our trip interesting. Finally, no one could doubt his courage, but he hardly seemed like a killing machine. To me, he just looked tired and a little dispirited by a hard life.

We reached the Rawlings ranch about four o'clock. Widow Rawlings reminded me of an oak tree—strong, solid, and weathered by a life of hardship. She looked to be in her mid-sixties, almost six feet tall, with gray hair, which she wore in a tight bun pulled tight on the back of her head. Mrs. Rawlings wore men's pants and a work shirt.

She insisted that Grandfather and I take a seat on the porch, and she bustled around the house for a few minutes before returning with two glasses of milk and a platter of oatmeal and raisin cookies. As soon as we finished the snack, she began worrying that she may have spoiled my supper.

"Don't worry about that, Loretta," Grandfather said with a wry smile. "From what I've heard, this boy can eat a whole apple pie and still make room for supper." Mrs. Rawlings looked puzzled. I just hung my head. I guessed I would never live down the incident with the pie.

Grandfather briefly repeated the story of my father's death to the sheriff's widow and invited her to the service. Loretta Rawlings cried, repeating over and over, "Poor Davey, poor, poor Davey," gently caressing my face with calloused hands.

"I was hoping that Brother Stumpy might conduct the

memorial," Grandfather interrupted. "Is he up at the bunkhouse?"

"Nope," she sniffed. "He's over at the church working on his Sunday sermon."

We said our goodbyes and headed back down the ranch road to the highway.

The church sat in a grove of ancient oaks. The small white frame building didn't look like it would accommodate fifty people, and the giant live oaks dwarfed the modest steeple. A tired horse wandered along the banks of a spring-fed pond, cropping grass and stopping occasionally to take long drinks from the clear, cool water.

At the sound of our truck, Brother Stumpy came to the door to greet his visitors. He hardly fit anyone's stereotype of a minister. He was an inch or two shorter than me, but wide and muscular. He appeared pretty old to me—at least forty-five or fifty. His face had the scarred and battered look of a bar fighter. Some of my father's Marine friends had the same look, with broken, flattened noses and cauliflower ears from innumerable drunken brawls. Brother Stumpy dressed like a cowman, his legs bowed by a lifetime spent in the saddle.

"Well, B-B-Brother Wallace," he stuttered. "What a p-pleasant s-s-surprise."

My grandfather shook hands warmly with the short cowman, then sat on the porch steps while Brother Stumpy took a seat in a ragged rocking chair. I leaned against the door of the truck, playing with Red's ears and watching the lazy horse munch grass.

After Grandfather told Stumpy about my father's death, he introduced me and explained about the memorial service he had planned. "Harley and I were hoping that you'd conduct the service," he concluded.

Tears glistened in the short parson's eyes. "I'd be h-honored," he said.

He took out a small spiral notebook from his shirt pocket and a stub of a pencil and jotted down information about my father. He asked a question or two, but mostly encouraged Grandfather and me to tell stories about favorite memories of my father. Brother Stumpy seemed lost in thought, his sad, battered face bathed in the light of the late afternoon sun.

After finalizing the details of the service and having a brief prayer, we headed toward Grandfather's ranch. We rode in silence for a few minutes. I was upset, and I guess it must have shown.

"You got something on your mind," Grandfather said. "Spit it out."

"Brother Stumpy stutters and looks like—he looks like a bar fighter. Are you sure he's the one to do the service for my dad?"

"Let me tell you something about Brother Stumpy. I suppose he got his nickname because he is built like a stump—short, wide, and gnarled like tree bark. Also, because his name is Ellis Crabtree."

Grandfather's eyes were on the road, his hands on the wheel, but he drove so slowly a trotting horse could have passed us. Clearly, his thoughts were on things other than driving.

"People have made a habit out of underestimating Brother Stumpy. His father did, and Stumpy almost killed the man for crippling his mother in a drunken rage. Sheriff Rawlings did, and Stumpy killed him. The prisoners at Raiford did, and he beat many of them to a bloody pulp. The warden put his name on a parole list, thinking he had no chance of being released, but again he beat the odds."

If my grandfather hoped the story would ease my mind, it wasn't working. It must have shown on my face.

"Now before you go making up your mind," Grandfather warned, "you need to hear the rest of his story."

"After Stumpy had been in prison three years, someone he'd beaten up drove a homemade knife through his chest while he slept. Everyone assumed he was a dead man, but again they underestimated him. In the infirmary, a lifer named Jarvis White took care of Stumpy. The prisoners called Jarvis "the Butcher," but he had found religion in prison, and I guess it's safe to say he saved Stumpy's life and his soul. Jarvis nursed Stumpy night and day, talking to him about redemption and repentance. Stumpy finally came out of the hospital ward a changed man. The anger in him had been replaced by love."

The truck crept along now, the wheels barely moving. I began wondering if walking wouldn't be faster.

"He won parole after twelve years and came back to Timucua County. It would have been easier to start life somewhere else, of course. Loretta Rawlings threatened to kill him with a shotgun, but again he survived. He worked for her without pay, hunting cattle in the swamps alone with nothing but the clothes on his back, his horse and saddle, and his Bible. He finally convinced her he had changed."

"A few years ago, Mrs. Rawlings gave him an acre of land to build his church. The first Sunday service, people packed the pews to see Stumpy fail. Everyone knew he stuttered. But when he spoke from the pulpit, he never missed a syllable."

We puttered along in silence for a few minutes while Grandfather collected his thoughts.

"I guess what I'm saying is, we all make mistakes. I messed up badly with raising your father, and you stole Sheriff McCully's pie. That is part of being human. I hope you'll give Brother Stumpy a chance. I know that he'll do a good job."

I still doubted that the stuttering minister would do justice to my father's memory, but I really didn't think I could second-guess the old man. One thing I'd learned from our few hours together, I felt confident that Grandfather wouldn't do anything to spoil the memorial to my father.

A mile or so before reaching the Dingle Ferry Bridge, Grandfather turned off the highway, following a pair of ruts which led through the darkening forest to the banks of the Wildcat. The sun was beginning to set. Eerie shadows from the oaks wavered in the fading light. The Wildcat shimmered in the gold and orange light of dusk, glowing like a sluggish river of flowing lava.

Grandfather Wallace's ranch house, and my new home, perched on a high hill perhaps a quarter of a mile south of the river. The dwelling had obviously once been a simple dogtrot cabin, the standard architecture of Cracker homes. When Great-Grandfather Wallace built it, the house simply consisted of two large rooms separated by an open hallway, which everyone called a dogtrot. As the family grew and made a little money, several additions had been made to the house. A loft room had been constructed to provide sleeping quarters for the children, and two rooms, in the shape of an "I," jutted off from the left room. Covered porches, front and rear, offered shade from the scorching Florida heat. The house had a tin roof, and handsawn, unpainted cypress boards covered the exterior.

Several ancient live oaks loomed over the house. Barns and outbuildings scattered, seemingly at random, surrounded the house. A large bunkhouse for the cowboys had been made by renovating the old, detached, brick kitchen. Horses and cattle wandered freely over the hill, munching contentedly on the lush grass.

The house wasn't very impressive for one of the largest cowmen in Florida. But it seemed to fit my grandfather. Like him, it was solid and rough-hewn.

"This is where my father first saw this land," my grandfather said softly. "I like to come here at twilight just to remember the old folks and watch the night come over the land."

We sat beside the Wildcat in silence for a few minutes watching the change of light. A flock of turkeys rose into a nearby sweetgum tree to roost. An owl hooted a warning to the night's small creatures that it had started its patrol.

"There's a ford here," Grandfather said. "I use it sometimes when the water level is low."

He eased the old truck out into the river, and the waters of the Wildcat never rose above the running boards. Red stuck his head out of the window, braying at a single heron clumsily taking wing into the setting sun. The cattle on the hill raised their heads in unison at the sound and then resumed their supper of winter grass.

Grandfather Wallace obviously lived in only one room, the combination kitchen and dining room. A few of Grandmother Wallace's feminine touches still remained. Lace curtains hung limply over the windows, and three delicate, light green cups sat on the windowsill. A picture of a vase of flowers, cut from a magazine and framed, and a painting of Jesus praying in the Garden of Gethsemane hung on the dining room wall.

From the looks of it, Grandfather had changed the room to fit his needs. He had pushed the table against the wall and put a daybed under the window. Uneven stacks of books and magazines littered the floor, with a few clear lanes left for movement among the stove, the door, and the bed. I saw copies of *Outdoor Life*, *American Legion*, and *Florida Cattleman* in the piles of periodicals, and the books seemed to be mostly history, a few Zane Gray novels, and publications on doctoring animals. Clothes lay where he had dropped them. A lamp stood at the head of the bed, and a radio sat on the mantel over the fireplace. An electric bulb hung suspended from its cord in the middle of the room, but when we came inside he lit a pair of kerosene lamps.

He looked around at the mess and shrugged. "I guess I've

lived alone too long," he said with a tired smile.

"Just lay your bag over there." He pointed toward the least cluttered corner.

Grandfather set water in a blackened pot on the wood stove to boil and then dug around in a barrel of salt, pulling out four large fish fillets. He expertly washed the salt off the fish, dumped a couple of cups of grits in the boiling water, and rolled the fish in corn meal. It took only about fifteen minutes to cook the meal.

"Pretty good," I said. I attacked the food like a bear just out of hibernation. I had never eaten grits with fish, but they made a tasty combination.

"They're mullet," he said, pointing at the fried fillets. "A lot of folks don't like them much because they have a mud strip. But most Floridians think of mullet when you mention seafood."

After supper, I washed the dishes while the old man straightened the room. When I could not stifle a yawn, Grandfather grabbed my valise and pointed me toward the stairs, following me up. A dark, spooky hallway led to the loft.

Grandfather opened the door to a dark room. He pulled on the string dangling from the bare light bulb, and I saw the most beautiful room I have ever seen. Neat and orderly shelves of books lined the walls. Portraits of General Lee and my grandfather's namesakes, General E. A. Perry and Colonel David Lang, hung over the bed. A large, unframed oil painting of the Great War had been nailed to the wall near the foot of the bed. Even before I read the signature, I knew that Captain Bobby Tate had painted the picture. In it, explosions ripped across No Man's Land, and doughboys with faces contorted in agony struggled toward the hidden enemy. I found it hard to believe that the same artist who created graceful, beautiful landscapes had painted this hellish scene.

"Do you like it?" Grandfather asked. "It was your dad's room."

I turned slowly in the middle of the room, imagining my father's spirit hovering nearby.

Grandfather bent down and fished a small trunk from under the bed. He set it on the cot and popped open the lid.

"This was your father's personal stuff. It's yours now. I know his whip and pistol are there. The gun is loaded, so be careful. Did Davey teach you how to use a handgun?"

I nodded. "He said I was pretty good."

"If he said that, I believe it." He walked back to the door. "Goodnight Harley. Now you go to bed soon—I know you're tired. And if you need anything, just holler."

I went through the trunk, finding articles and pictures, clothes, and the assorted junk that boys seem to always accumulate. I found an article about my grandfather's heroics in France from *American Legion* and several newspaper accounts of the battle with the Tuttle gang carefully preserved in wax paper. A little .32 H&S revolver lay in a well-oiled holster atop his carefully folded clothes, and I found a whip coiled in the bottom of the case.

Exploring my father's old room would have taken many hours, but after a while, I put the trunk aside and stretched out on the bed. I was almost asleep when a soft, plaintive sound began to whisper through the Florida night. I peeked out the window. In the shadows I saw Grandfather Wallace had propped a chair against the porch wall and was softly playing a fiddle. The music, as old as the Highlands of Scotland and as sad as its history, wafted over the sand hills like the lament of a fallen angel. I listened, crying quietly, until I finally drifted off into a dreamless sleep.

5

Life, Death, and Everything in Between

L ife on the ranch followed a well-established routine. Grandfather's two cowmen, Gaspar and John, usually came to breakfast before sunup. They ate eggs, bacon or ham, and biscuits at the kitchen table and mumbled over steaming cups of black coffee about what they would do that day. Most afternoons, they did not return to the ranch until after dark.

The two old cowmen were both tall and lean but there the similarities ended. John had all the personality of a bowl of pudding, but his loyalty to the Wallace family was unswerving. He never shied away from the hard, dirty work, and he seldom talked to me except to warn me to keep away from "them loose women in Tampa." More than once, Grandfather suggested that he follow his own advice.

Gaspar, on the other hand, had a lively sense of humor and sang with a disconcerting country twang. Give him a pair of *bolas* and *vaquero* pants and he could have starred in *Song of the Pampas* or one of those other silly Argentine Westerns. He had been called Gaspar for so long that few remembered his real name. He was like a brother to my grandfather.

The day after we arrived at the ranch, Grandfather began my education as a cowman. First, we roped up horses and he taught me to ride. We covered miles each day, doctoring animals, mending fences, and checking for signs of rustlers or danger-ous animals. During our travels we talked about everything except the men he had killed.

Once I asked the old man about school, but he seemed totally unconcerned about my attending the local one-room school. I knew he valued learning though. He insisted that I read history or a novel every evening, and we both read every newspaper we could get our hands on.

"Can you read and add, subtract, multiply, and divide?" he asked.

"Of course. I was in the eighth grade at Beaufort."

"Well, then, everything else you need to know you can learn from reading. If there is any book you want, I'll get it for you."

We almost always got to the ranch an hour before sundown. Together we would fish in the Wildcat or shoot tin cans off of fence posts. Some days he rarely spoke, and Grandfather did not easily tolerate my foolishness. One morning when I hid a coachwhip snake in John's boots, he almost whipped me. Still, I began to understand how much he cared for me and how much like him my father had been.

"This summer we'll go fish for a week on Lake Seminole," he promised one afternoon as we cast for bluegills in the Wildcat. "I got some friends at Pigbone who'll lend us a boat."

Pigbone, he explained, was a town of black people located on the northern shore of Lake Seminole. They distrusted most white people, and most whites pretended that Pigbone didn't exist. "The only reason a white boy would ever go there," John once warned me, "is if he is looking for bad women or a fight." Grandfather didn't seem to share John's misgivings about Pigbone.

All work ceased on Sunday. Gaspar disappeared and John slept late and rode into Peru Landing. I read and napped after a big noon meal, and Grandfather and I listened to the radio news reports. I asked him if I needed to do anything for the memorial service, but he shook his head. "If it ain't done by now," he said, "it ain't worth doing on the Lord's Day."

The day scheduled for my father's memorial service dawned bright and unseasonably warm, but that was about the only thing that went right on the day of the ceremony. I have heard the old-timers say, "Man plans and God laughs." It's true. Life has a way of disrupting our plans.

I can't blame Brother Stumpy. He was eloquent. He presented a message full of positive, hopeful sentiments and stories of my father's youth. He related how my father saved a playmate from drowning, and how he camped for a week in the swamp, without fire or tent, while hunting a panther that had been killing Grandfather's cattle. I'd never heard any of these stories.

Brother Stumpy read the scriptures promising resurrection for those who die in the Lord. The gnarled minister ended the service with a poem from the Great War:

"They shall not grow old as we who are left grow old.
Age shall not wither them, nor the years condemn,
But at the setting of the sun, and in the morning
We shall remember them."

More than two hundred people had gathered at the ranch for the memorial service. I cried like a baby—and I didn't care who saw it.

I'm told that Irishmen drink at their wakes for the dead. Southerners eat to drown their sorrow. The tables groaned under the weight of the food brought by the ladies of Timucua County. Every edible vegetable common to the area had been lovingly cooked for the feast. A whole table held nothing but casseroles, the duckbill platypus of the food world.

Grandfather Wallace provided the meat—a "fatted calf"—barbequed over a pit of hickory wood. Some of the men probably did some drinking too, but they kept their bottles a discreet distance from the women and children.

I did my best to make sure that none of the ladies who brought food felt slighted. When I went back for a third helping, Grandfather, Brother Stumpy, and Mrs. Rawlings shook their heads in disbelief and wandered off in different directions to meet and greet the friends.

After gorging myself, I went off to find my grandfather. He stood on the hill near the family cemetery, closely watching the Wildcat, a sparkling line glistening in the sunlight as it meandered toward the Gulf. I didn't say anything to him. Frowning, he nervously paced back and forth, his gaze locked on the far bend in the river. I sat down quietly nearby, with my back against a live oak tree. After a while, he came and squatted on his haunches near me.

"Something wrong?" I asked.

"My sister Rosie and the Manigaults didn't show up for the service. And, Gaspar hasn't come back either."

I already knew he was upset with Gaspar. John and I had caught the sharp edge of his tongue on that subject at breakfast. Gaspar had been dating a widow near the county line. He spent each Sunday with her and rarely got back before midnight.

When John had come to the kitchen for breakfast, he announced that Gaspar had not gotten back yet. "I guess Gaspar finally got lucky," John said.

"How did he get lucky?" I asked, as innocent as you please.

John burst out laughing, but after a quick glance at my grandfather, he grabbed his coffee, fried ham, and biscuits and retreated to the bunkhouse. I wound up getting the lecture on talking dirty and keeping promises. My father used to give me the same speech, word for word.

I decided not to mention Gaspar again for a while.

"Maybe Aunt Rosie misunderstood the time or day," I suggested.

"Nope. Captain Bobby said she knew exactly when the service would be held. I cain't figure she'd miss the service for Davey unless they've got big trouble."

He picked at the ground with a twig, idly making long grooves in the black loam, his mind miles away, and his brow furrowed. I could tell that he wanted to go search for his missing family and friends, but good manners dictated that he couldn't ask his guests to go home or leave them long without a host.

I said, "Would you like me to take a horse and go look for them?"

He thought about that for a while and shook his head. "The water is calm and there ain't a better man with a boat on the west coast of Florida than Norman Manigault."

After a while Grandfather stood up and tossed away his stick. "I reckon we ought to go down and see about our company."

John met us at the bottom of the hill. He had taken off his coat and tie, but sweat plastered his shirt to his body and glistened on his face. The lean cowboy tried to smile at me, but he looked like he was about ready to burst into tears.

"I see you a minute, boss?"

"Just spit it out, John. The boy will know anything we say in five minutes anyway."

"Gaspar's horse came in a few minutes ago. The saddle is covered in blood. I'm taking my horse and backtracking to the county line."

A momentary look of shock crossed my grandfather's face as the news sank in. The look quickly became one of rage. Gaspar and he had been friends for forty years. When my father ran off and joined the Marines, Gaspar had left a job as a government cattle inspector to return and ease Grandfather through the harsh and sorrowful times. He was like a brother to the old man, and the code in those days still required that the death of kin must be avenged with blood.

Grandfather shook his head. "No. Let's do this right. Get ten horses from the pasture. We'll put together a search party. I want to leave in fifteen minutes so we don't lose the afternoon light."

Brother Stumpy took charge of selecting the men. A few of the men chosen for the posse had saddles with them in the back of their Model T's or wagons, and the rest got what they needed from the storeroom. All but the short minister had some type of gun with them. Most of the men simply took off their coats and replaced their shoes with work boots. After taking off the ridiculous tie, I took my father's old pistol and a handful of shells and put them in my saddlebags.

Leaning against the rough gatepost of the corral, just outside the circle of men, I listened as the gossip began. A tall man named Johnson leaned on a post near me, working a wad of tobacco the size of a hen's egg in his cheek. There is a know-it-all in every group, and Johnson seemed to believe himself the expert on any subject that came up.

"Had to be a panther or a stranger," he announced to the group.

"How do you figure that?" asked an elderly cowhand who had arrived with Mrs. Rawlings.

"Well, the bears ain't got cubs this early in the season, so they wouldn't attack a human. A panther is the only creature big enough, and smart enough, to injure Gaspar."

"Okay," the old cowboy agreed. "But why a stranger?"

"Only a stranger to the area would risk making an enemy of Perry Wallace. You remember what happened to . . ."

I leaned forward, definitely interested to learn more on this subject, but Brother Stumpy interrupted.

"King David once s-said, 'I was s-s-silent, not knowing what to s-say.' I've found that to be p-pretty good advice." He didn't look at Johnson, but the grins on the men's faces showed that the barb had hit its mark.

Brother Stumpy came over and crouched next to me. John brought up the horses a few minutes later, and we got busy saddling up for what promised to be a long ride. Several of the women wrapped food in brown butcher paper and stuffed the provisions in cloth bags for the search party. Mrs. Rawlings loaded a double-sized parcel for me.

We mounted and Grandfather, and Brother Stumpy were giving last minute instructions when Red came out from under the hydrangea near the front porch steps and began to whine. He'd been in dog heaven—lying in the shade, surrounded by a mound of bones. I figured that it would take something important to get him stirring. The low whimpering noise lasted only a few seconds. The hound burst across the yard, through a gap in the tables, and headed for the hill overlooking the Wildcat, his bell-like bark echoing through the high hills and woods.

Everyone turned to look, for the old dog had never raised a false alarm. He returned a minute or two later followed by Great Aunt Rosie and Norman and Florry Manigault. A pretty blonde-haired girl, wearing a dark blue dress, trailed behind the old folks.

Grandfather slipped off his horse and rushed over to hug his sister. They whispered together, grim-faced and solemn. I watched my grandfather carefully, trying to get some indication of what was happening. Aunt Rosie did most of the talking, and I could tell by Grandfather's expression that she had not brought good news. The rest of the search party sat in patient silence.

Grandfather directed the newcomers over to the tables of food and walked, dejected and sloop-shouldered, to where we sat.

"The Manigaults found Gaspar's body floating at the mouth of the Wildcat. He'd been shot," he announced. A flurry of shouted questions followed, but my grandfather offered little additional information.

"I really appreciate your help," he told the searchers. "I'd like John and Brother Stumpy to backtrack Gaspar's horse, and maybe find out where the killing occurred. The sheriff will take over from here, but I'll spread the word when we get more information."

When the last of the guests had departed and Aunt Rosie and the Manigaults had finished eating, Norman and I cleaned up the area and put away the sawhorses and planks that had served as tables. Norman Manigault was lean, not much taller than me, and about fifteen years younger than my grandfather. Sun, wind, and storm had tanned his face like old leather.

"You Davey's boy?" he asked after the others had retired to the front porch.

I nodded.

"Sorry to hear about his death. He had a rough life, but he was a good man. The sheriff kept us at the Landing for questioning or we would have been here to pay our respects."

After we got everything in order, we joined the others on the porch. Red had taken a position near the blonde girl. She was very pretty. I went over to sit by the old hound.

We were close enough to hear Aunt Rosie in the middle of her narrative of the trip from Bear Paw Island to the memorial service. The stout, old lady wore tiny spectacles that flashed in the afternoon sun. Despite her sad news, Aunt Rosie's face radiated an aura of good humor. It appeared that she had received all the playfulness in the family, while Grandfather received all the solemnity.

"It was a fluke," she continued, "pure and simple. We got an early start. Nothing would have kept us from Davey's memorial. We had smooth water, and we were just starting to catch the current of the Wildcat when Beth yelled, 'Stop! I see something over there.' I swear that girl got old Commodore Boaz's sharp eyesight. I looked over to where she was pointing and didn't see anything. But Norman decided we needed to check it out. I'm sure glad we did."

Beth—the blonde girl—fidgeted nervously. She obviously did not like being the center of attention.

"You remember that old Greek from Tarpon Springs who spent all summer cutting cedar trees out of the Tyler Fort Swamp? That was two years ago, I think. Then he floated them logs up to the pencil factories at Cedar Key. He had ten or twelve rafts lashed together, but he obviously lost a few logs along the way. Gaspar's shirt got snagged on a cedar trunk about a quarter of a mile from shore. Like I said—just a fluke. If he hadn't gotten his shirt hooked on that snag, he would have been fish food, and we would never have found the body."

She stopped, folding her chubby hands in her lap, as if giving her audience a chance to ponder the ironies of fate.

"You sure he was shot?" Grandfather asked.

"Oh yes. Shot from behind." She hesitated. "The bullet went in the back of his skull and came out the front. I never saw anything quite like it before . . . terrible . . . terrible!"

There was another long pause before she continued.

"Anyway, we pulled into the Landing, and Norman got Mr. Levy's clerk to let him use the phone to call the sheriff. Took him an hour to get there from Lewisburg and another two hours to ask us all the same questions over and over. I really think that stupid man would have charged one of us with murder if he thought he could get away with it."

Aunt Rosie had obviously found a subject she could get her teeth into, and she went after it like a pack of hounds on a grounded coon.

"I always knew that Warren Messer was lazy, white trash. And I'll remember the way he treated us come Election Day. Just goes to show you, put a badge on trash and you still got trash. Only thing is, he thinks putting a shiny star on his chest automatically makes him a Wyatt Earp."

I'd heard enough. I stood up, stretched like I had a cramp, and wandered off down the hillside to the family cemetery. I didn't mean to be rude, but I'd heard enough talk of death to do me for a week.

Beth and Red followed me a few minutes later. The old dog came over and nudged me with his nose and licked at my hand. The girl crouched down beside me, hooking her arms around her knees. One of the rough boys in Beaufort told me that girls do that so boys can't see up their skirts, but I don't know if that's true.

"I was sure sorry to hear about your father," she said. "Aunt Rosie said he was a brave man."

I nodded, but didn't say anything. I felt that anyone who had not really known my father could never truly understand the depth of my loss.

"I wish Aunt Rosie hadn't made me wear this old dress, and I could sit by you and Red. Aunt Rosie said it wasn't proper to come to a funeral in work clothes."

"Yeah," I said. "Grandfather made me wear a tie." I pulled the red and black strip of cloth out of my pocket to show her. "I took it off when we were getting ready to go search for Gaspar."

Beth's long yellow hair shimmered in the afternoon sun and a few freckles dotted her nose and cheeks. Her eyes were the color of a cloudless sky. She seemed a little sad and serious most of the time, but when she gave a shy smile, her face lit up with an inner joy that banished the mask of sadness.

"Where is your stepmom? I haven't seen her."

"She got real drunk when she heard about my dad being

killed, and ran off." I started to say, "Good riddance to bad rubbish," but instead just muttered, "No great loss."

"I know how it feels to lose your family. Aunt Rosie said my mom died giving birth when I was three. The baby died, and my dad started drinking. He died a few months later from a bad batch of moonshine. I don't remember either of them. My mother was a second cousin to Commodore Manigault, Aunt Rosie's husband. Aunt Rosie and Uncle Norman and Aunt Flory took me in."

"Yeah, life stinks sometimes."

"Oh, I think we're both pretty lucky. I couldn't ask for a better family than Aunt Rosie and Uncle Norman. And Uncle Perry has sure surprised everyone. He must really love you. He has such a reputation around here for being a hard man, I never knew he could be so kind."

She was right. I hated to admit it, but the last week had been better than I imagined. In fact, I loved my life on the ranch and the old man. I'd been mired in a pit of self-pity, looking at my problems rather than counting my blessings. That is always a mistake. Beth gave me a smile, and I began to feel better about the hand life had dealt me.

Brother Stumpy and John came back to the ranch an hour or so after dark, tired, wet, and splattered with mud. They had lost the trail of Gaspar's horse near Widow Woman Slough.

Grandfather surprised me. He didn't seem upset by the news or even concerned. He made arrangements to give the two men a supper of leftovers, and outlined the sleeping arrangements for the night. Despite a few weak protests from the ladies, he decided that they would spend the night in the house, with its more luxurious accommodations. The men would sleep in the bunkhouse. Since Norman and Florry were the only married couple, the plan made perfect sense to me.

As soon as the women retired, Grandfather called a meeting of the men. A wind whispered in from the Gulf, and only a single lantern, guttering in the breeze, cast an eerie light in the center of the room.

"Gaspar was like a brother to me. He was my friend for forty years, and I want to get the person who shot him so bad I can taste it. But first, I must keep a promise I made to him." He paused, looking at the lantern.

"In the morning Harley and I are going to reclaim the body and drive it down to Tampa. Gaspar's brother is a priest there—Father Antonio Guzman. Gaspar always wanted to be buried in hallowed ground and have his brother conduct the funeral service. Harley and I are going to see that he is buried the way he wanted. Then, I'm going to come back and find the dirty . . . the man who murdered my friend."

The men talked for a few minutes, unrolling blankets and jabbering about the small things that they would do tomorrow. Grandfather took John aside, giving him final instructions for running the ranch in our absence.

I fell asleep almost before my head hit the pillow. I dreamed of an angel with yellow hair whose wistful smile could heal a battered soul.

A hint of first light shimmered on the morning sky when I awoke in the dark bunkhouse. My grandfather stood at the bunkhouse door, already dressed, staring south toward Widow Woman Slough. Watching him in the light of the rising sun, I realized he didn't look dangerous, but like a very sad and weary old man.

6

Government Business

We spent two days in Tampa getting Gaspar properly buried. I thought that we'd leave for Timucua County following the funeral, but Grandfather announced that we would be spending the night at the church.

"Father Antonio says he needs to speak with us," he explained.

The old priest provided a tiny room in the church to store our gear and sleep. A monk who took seriously his vow of poverty must have furnished the cell. It had two narrow cots, an unpainted pine table, and a simple wooden cross nailed to a wall. The only source of light came from a candle and a small, square window located so high in the wall that the last occupant of the room must have been a descendant of Goliath.

Father Antonio took no time to grieve for his younger brother, but attended to his duty to his flock. I tired of sitting in the pews of Our Lady of Nueva Esperanza (which Grandfather said meant New Hope) and went and sat on a slight hill behind the church's garden. From there, I could see the ships entering and leaving Tampa Bay under a darkening sky.

All evening a steady stream of women and elderly men came out of the church into the garden to kneel by a statue of Mary and baby Jesus, making the sign of the cross and fingering their rosaries. When some of the women cried and made soft wailing noises, a young priest would appear to hold the mourner's hand and whisper words of comfort.

A pitch black night had settled over the city of Tampa before Father Antonio finally came into the garden. He limped along slowly, like a man carrying a great burden. A few candles by the statue illuminated the garden, their tiny flames guttering in the sea breeze. I moved closer to the priest and sat beside a small concrete pool covered with water hyacinths. Grandfather soon joined us, taking his seat on the marble bench beside Gaspar's brother.

After a minute or so, Father Antonio spoke in a tired monotone. "With so many sons going off to war," he said, "many of our members seem to have become more regular in their worship and confessions."

The two old men discussed the war news. Each new day seemed to bring some new disaster for the Allies. No one seemed capable of halting the Japanese rampage through the Pacific. The British were buying time, on two fronts, with their blood and guts, but the outlook appeared dismal. Emperor Hirohito's forces had just captured the seventy-thousand-man English garrison in Singapore. Grandfather believed the Japanese would move quickly south to conquer Australia and the American army in the Philippines. In North Africa, a German general named Rommel applied the speed and mobility of the Confederate cavalry to tank warfare, winning victory after victory over the gritty British soldiers. Grandfather called them "Tommies." Father Antonio said he thought the United States seemed on the verge of panic. Californians braced for an invasion by the Japanese, and off the East Coast packs of German U-Boats lurked along the shipping lanes, destroying supplies and war materials meant for our European allies.

The two old men sat in silence for a few minutes, each occupied with his own thoughts.

Father Antonio finally spoke, his voice almost a whisper. "The reason I asked you to stay was to give you a message from the Widow Price. She and Gaspar were courting, but you already knew that."

"She seems like a nice lady. I think Gaspar really liked her."

The priest nodded. He hesitated, as if choosing his words with great care. "Widow Price told me that Gaspar thought that something strange was going on near the county line."

"Did she say what?"

"No. She said Gaspar was going to talk to you about hiring a couple of reliable men to patrol the southern part of your ranch and the area around Ortiz Point. She said that they always listened to a music program on the radio before he started back to the ranch. You know, big bands, that sort of thing. But on the afternoon he died, the widow said he couldn't get settled down and left early. Gaspar said he needed to check something before it got too dark."

Grandfather got up and began pacing. He asked a few more questions, but the priest didn't seem to know anything more about the death of his brother.

The sounds of a stevedore cursing as he helped unload a freighter drifted up from the distant harbor. I suddenly felt homesick for the ranch. In a few days it had become my home. I missed the keening cry of the night birds and the soft rustle of a night breeze in the Spanish moss. I longed for the comfort of my father's room, the sound of grazing cattle moving to fresh grass at first light, and the gentle splash of fish moving into the shallows of the Wildcat.

I watched my grandfather walking slowly back and forth, and it dawned on me how much I loved this scarred old man. People said he was a hard man. Some people feared him. I knew he had a dark, dangerous streak in him, but I had finally realized that he cared for me and would never intentionally hurt me.

Grandfather finally quit pacing and came and sat beside the priest.

"Gaspar never gave me a bum steer," he said. "I just wish I knew what he saw that made him suspicious."

"I asked the Widow Price, but she didn't seem to know any more than what I told you."

Grandfather nodded. He seemed to have decided on a course of action.

He asked Father Antonio, "Does the church have a phone I can use? I need to make a few calls."

"Of course."

I got up to go with him, but Grandfather told me that I needed to attend to my studies. He had insisted that I bring my volume of Ridpath's *History of the World* dealing with the Crusades.

"I don't think there's going to be any late breaking news on that subject," I observed. "Besides, I know how it ends. The Christians take Jerusalem, they lose Jerusalem, and if they found the Holy Grail, no one knows it."

Father Antonio laughed at my impudence, but quickly averted his face. My grandfather only stared at me, then turned to follow the priest to the church offices. We all knew the old man's sudden interest in my education was just a handy excuse to get me out of the way for a while.

Father Antonio got Grandfather a desk and telephone book and walked me back to the room. The old priest appeared pensive and distracted. I assumed his concerns centered on finding Gaspar's murderer.

"Grandfather will find and kill Gaspar's killer," I assured him.

"No, no, no. God will take care of those who killed my brother. 'Vengeance is mine, I will repay, saith the Lord.' Your grandfather has other concerns right now, I suspect."

"Well, I think Grandfather intends to be God's little

helper here on earth."

Father Antonio ignored my attempt at sarcasm. "Right now, I'm more concerned with your attitude than Perry Wallace's." The priest leaned against a dark wall. "Your grandfather is a hard man who has seen more than his share of trouble. He has tried to live according to what he thinks is right. Along the way he has made mistakes. Young people think that adults should be perfect. That, we can never be. Try not to be too hard on him."

I understood what he was trying to tell me. Grandfather said the same thing when he finished his Brother Stumpy story. We all make mistakes. We learn from them, correct them as best we can, and go on.

The old priest stopped by the kitchen and found me some cookies and a glass of milk. I took them back to the room, determined to stay awake until my grandfather returned.

Grandfather shook me awake at dawn. He had packed his bags and made his bed, if he slept on it at all. "We gotta go," he said. "We're meeting an old buddy of mine at the ranch in three hours. He's a general in the army now. He led a Marine brigade during the Great War, and he's a man I can trust."

Grandfather usually drove a lot slower than my father, but he put the gas pedal to the floor as we sped north out of Tampa. A million questions flashed through my mind, but I didn't say anything. I didn't want him taking his eyes off the road or his hands off the wheel. Instead, I watched the soft, liquid beauty of the Florida landscape materialize in the early morning light, listening as the *thump thump* of the tires on the hard road changed to a gentle *slap slap* when the pavement ended. Even on the packed clay trail, Grandfather kept the old truck flying.

General Oliver Hazard Bullard arrived at the ranch less than ten minutes after we got home. He knew how to make an entrance. A sleek, new olive-green roadster came roaring down the dirt road trailing a thick cloud of dust. The driver hit the brakes and spun to a stop near the porch in a hail of gravel and rock.

The driver, a sour-faced little corporal named Sullivan, hopped out, ran around to open the back door, and saluted as General Bullard got out. The general looked to be a little older than my grandfather. He stood ramrod straight, six feet three inches of muscle and gristle, and as hard as tempered steel. His close-cropped hair was sprinkled with gray, but it made him look distinguished, not old.

"*Semper fi*, General," Grandfather said, using the standard greeting of Marine veterans.

"*Semper fi*, Lieutenant."

Turning to his driver, the general nodded in the direction of my grandfather. "Corporal Sullivan, this is Perry Wallace. He served with me in France during the Great War. Perry Wallace is the bravest man I ever knew. I put him up for the Congressional Medal of Honor, but he had to settle for a DSC and a cigar box full of Frenchie medals."

"Corporal, welcome to my home," Grandfather said.

The pinch-faced little soldier snapped to attention and saluted. When the two old friends turned, I thought I saw the young soldier smirk. Instinctively, I did not like the man.

Grandfather nudged me up in front of the general and introduced me. The general shook my hand and said, "Nice to meet you Harley. I was so sorry to learn about your father. I served with him in Nicaragua during the thirties. He was a fine Marine."

That was, I know he believed, the highest of compliments.

With the introductions completed, General Bullard turned to his driver and snapped, "Get my briefcase and stay by the car. Lieutenant Wallace and I have some important matters to discuss."

I headed down to the corral, saddled a horse, and went out in the south pastures to find John and Brother Stumpy. I figured they would be working a herd of cattle down near Panther Hammock, putting ointment on the animals' cuts and scratches to keep away the screwworms. The foul-smelling medicine was clear when first applied, but quickly changed to a bright purple. It smelled a lot like vinegar that had spoiled. No cowman liked the nasty but necessary task of treating cattle for screwworms.

The Texas tick epidemics had nearly destroyed the Florida cattle herds during the years around the Great War. That plague ended when ranchers began giving their cattle periodic dips in vats filled with tick poison. Screwworms had appeared shortly after that, and they were much worse. Those parasites laid their eggs in open wounds in cattle. When the eggs hatched, the larvae ate away the flesh of the unfortunate creatures until it died in agony—a walking skeleton. Any untreated cut became a cow's death sentence.

I told the two cowboys about our trip to Tampa while we worked. News of the general's visit to the ranch obviously interested them, but they were too polite to pry for information. I had no clue what the two old comrades were discussing, but I did not want John and Brother Stumpy to know I was as much in the dark as they were.

We worked until noon. While the two men took a break for a few bites of cornbread and salt pork, Brother Stumpy asked me to ride back to the shed behind the barn for a five-gallon bucket of the purple ointment. They had been working in the hot sun since daylight, and I knew they would use the break to take a quick siesta in the shade.

When I got to the barn, I saw Corporal Sullivan leaning against the hood of the roadster, chain smoking cigarettes and slapping at sand gnats and mosquitoes. Having to cool his heels for so long had obviously worn his small supply of patience to the breaking point.

I hurried about my business and had no intention of talking to the dour little man. After several hours of boredom, I must have looked like an easy target. As I rode by he said, "So this is how a great war hero lives down here?"

"Yeah, it's pretty neat, ain't it," I replied. I could tell by the tone of his voice that he considered my home a rat hole.

Corporal Sullivan scratched a large welt on his neck and lit another cigarette. "Oh, sure. Going to an outhouse is so-o-o modern."

"Where do people use the bathroom where you come from, Corporal? The bedroom floor?"

"We have indoor toilets," he said, with some pride.

He slapped again, took a long drag on his smoke, and started scratching the back of his hand. January is one of the two months that pass for winter in Florida. The recent unseasonable heat had brought out a few of the pests, but none of the swarms that April and May would bring. I had barely noticed them at all, but they seemed to be driving the young corporal insane.

"The great war hero. Living like some Cracker sharecropper. No electricity, no telephone, scratching bugs and vermin, and probably eating nothing but cornpone and grits. Ain't that just neat?"

His attitude made me angry, but I tried to keep an "aw shucks" expression on my face. He seemed quite content to believe me a stupid hick.

"The bugs bothering you?" I asked just as innocently as you please.

He stopped scratching and slapping, peering at me like I had asked the stupidest question in the entire history of mankind.

"You don't notice me or anyone from around these parts being bothered by insects, do you?" I leaned forward, lowering my voice. "That's because we know the secret."

"What secret?"

"Why, for keeping bugs off, of course."

"How do you do that?"

"Salve."

"What salve?"

"It's called Bugsaway." I reached down in my saddlebags and pulled out a small squirt can of screwworm medicine. (Cowmen always carried a small amount of the ointment with them, in case they ran into a stray that needed doctoring.) "Just rub it on your face and hands and neck. You won't be troubled with bugs for days."

He took it gratefully, slathering large amounts of it over his exposed flesh. I watched, knowing I should leave before his skin turned purple. I just couldn't go. Call it scientific curiosity. In truth, I wanted to see his reaction when he realized an ignorant Cracker child had fooled him. I slipped off my horse and climbed into the lower limbs of a nearby water oak.

Corporal Sullivan lit another cigarette and leaned against the automobile, content at last. When he finished his smoke, he dropped the butt on the ground and reached into his pocket for another cigarette. That's when he noticed that his hands were the color of ripe plums.

He screeched like a man bitten by a snake. He whirled around, saw his reflection in the car window, and went totally berserk. He grabbed a thick board from a nearby stack of lumber and began poking at my dangling feet.

I started climbing, but he landed a lucky blow on my left leg, dislodging me from my perch. I squalled as I fell, landing with a hard thud on the exposed roots near the trunk of the tree. The fall knocked the wind out of me. I lay there stunned, unable to move, as the purple soldier raised the plank to strike.

"Corporal Sullivan!"

We both jerked around in the direction of the shout. The driver dropped the board and snapped to attention. General Bullard stood a few feet away, hands on his hips. Grandfather Wallace crouched nearby in a shooting stance, a .38 pistol only inches from the corporal's ear. I had never realized before that Grandfather wore a shoulder holster. The look on the old man's grim and angry face left no doubt that he desperately wanted to kill the little soldier.

"Corporal," the general said in a quiet, even voice, "you are about one second away from being dead. Would you please explain to Lieutenant Wallace why you are attacking his grandson?" He hesitated briefly and continued. "And explain to me why, in God's name, you have painted yourself purple."

"It's all his fault!" he screamed, pointing at me. "It's all . . ."

The sound of Grandfather cocking that .38 brought his tirade to an abrupt halt. It is amazing how loud a small click can sound in the proper situation. I also noticed, for the first time, that Red had positioned himself in front of me, fangs bared and a low growl rumbling deep in his chest.

"Corporal," the general said, "before my friend Perry has to kill you, and I have to help hide your body, why don't you get into that car. I'll apologize to Harley for you.'

"Apologize to . . ."

"One more word, Mr. Sullivan, and you'll find yourself the private in charge of giving oral exams to polar bears in Greenland. Now, get in that car!"

The poor soldier, sputtering incoherently and with the veins of his neck bulging out, scurried over to the roadster and slammed the door. He looked at his face in the rear view mirror and started pounding on the window and screaming with rage.

General Bullard shook his head. "How are we going to make an army with idiots like Sullivan?"

"We did it in seventeen," Grandfather said quietly.

"Yeah. I guess you're right." He shook his head as if visualizing an army of drooling imbeciles. "Well, I'll send you the equipment we talked about. Also the gas voucher. They'll start rationing fuel before long. If you need anything else, or have important intelligence, call that private number I gave you."

The two old comrades warmly shook hands, and the general got in his automobile. Corporal Sullivan gunned the engine, fishtailed the car into the ruts, and scratched off in a cloud of dust.

"He acts like he's anxious to leave," I said in a deadpan voice.

"Harley, I told you before—you have a dangerous sense of humor," Grandfather groused, shaking his head. "But I suppose things will never be dull here with you around."

I thought Grandfather might give me a hint as to what he and the general discussed, but he made me tell him what happened with Corporal Sullivan as we jogged our horses to help John and Brother Stumpy.

"He kept making fun of us," I said after relating the tale.

"I figured it must have been something like that."

"You and my dad have done more for this country than he'll ever do if he lives a hundred years. You'd think he'd show some respect."

"No. There are people in the so-called seats of power who really believe people in the South and West are a bunch of rubes and bumpkins. They call us hillbillies, felt hat boys, hicks, and Crackers. The only time they want to admit we have value is when they have a war to fight. Then its 'rally round the flag, boys.'"

We rode on in silence until we finally found John and Brother Stumpy. When I rode off looking for strays, I heard the three men laughing, and I knew that my grandfather was telling them about the purple soldier.

After supper, Grandfather asked me to get my atlas from my room. I loved that book of maps. Using it, I could daydream of distant lands I would someday visit and locate the site of battles we heard about on the news. He cleared a space on the dining table and pulled up two chairs.

"I realize that you want to know what's happening in Timucua County," he said. "You've had the good manners to let me think things over without asking a lot of questions. But the fact is, I'm going to need your help. I'll tell you what I can."

He stopped talking for a moment, choosing his words carefully. "What I am going to tell you must remain a secret. You cannot tell anyone! Be very careful around strangers. Do you understand?"

I nodded. I felt very grown-up and important.

"Have you ever heard of a place called Takoradi?" he asked.

"No. It sounds Japanese."

"That's what I thought. But it's actually a town over in Africa."

Grandfather ran his finger along the map showing the west coast of Africa, until locating it just south of the Equator on the Atlantic Ocean in the British colony called the Gold Coast. Takoradi didn't look like much of a town. Major cities like London, New York, and Tokyo had their own colors on the maps, but only a tiny dot on the map indicated the location of the dusty African village.

"What in the world does a little town in Africa have to do with Florida?" To my way of thinking, it didn't make much sense.

"You know that President Roosevelt has been sending planes and military supplies to England and Russia for almost a year. The Lend-Lease Program."

I nodded. The papers had been full of that even before Pearl Harbor. German bombing attacks on England had destroyed so many British factories that they could no longer supply the planes and ships to fight a two-front war. President Roosevelt and Prime Minister Winston Churchill had signed an agreement to help each other. The British would buy military supplies from American factories and pay after the war. Some of the president's enemies had claimed Roosevelt was just giving the planes and ships to the Brits until he could find an excuse for entering the war.

"Okay. With the German fleet patrolling the North Atlantic and blocking safe passage to England, how would you get military equipment to our allies?"

"Go around them."

"Exactly. And that brings us to Takoradi."

Using a pencil, Grandfather traced a line from north Florida to Brazil, across the South Atlantic to Takoradi, and from there, north to Russia and England.

"Somewhere south of here, between Peru Landing and Tampa, the government has built a huge airfield. That base is the jump-off point for the planes being sent to Brazil. It's supposed to be totally secret. But when I called General Bullard with news that Gaspar thought he had seen something strange happening at Ortiz Point, his intelligence officers began worrying that there might have been a breach in security."

I found it hard to believe. Nazi spies creeping around in the hammocks and palmettos of Florida's Wildcat Bay region seemed ludicrous at first blush. Nothing important to the nation ever happened there. Yet, somehow it made perfect sense to me. I guessed that Gaspar might have stumbled upon enemy agents and been killed.

"The general wants us to establish a coast watch unit to keep an eye on our region. We are supposed to find out whether there are spies or saboteurs in the area, and if so, where is their base of operations. He's sending several radios, transmitters, and receivers, to allow the watchers to be in constant contact with us.

"Well," I said, "why doesn't the General just send the Marines into the area?"

"Two reasons. First, a military unit parading through the area would alert everyone in west Florida to the presence of a base. Can you imagine the field day the local gossips would have with Leathernecks trudging through the piney woods? They'd start poking their noses where they definitely don't belong. Secondly, we know the area better than they ever will. We will know a stranger or anything that seems out of place."

I nodded. That made sense to me.

Taking a sheet of paper from a notepad, Grandfather drew a rough outline of Timucua County. He put four "x" marks on the sketch: one at Ortiz Point, one at Bear Paw Island, one at Mr. Ollis' Sawmill, and the last one at the ranch.

"In order to get the network established, we need observation stations at these points," Grandfather said, tapping the four "x" marks. "I'm sending you over to Bear Paw to set up the listening post there. I'll send Stumpy to Ollis' and John and I will head down to Ortiz Point. Time is of the essence. A couple of swabbies are coming to Bear Paw, day after tomorrow, to set up the radios and antenna. We've got to be ready when they arrive. You need to pack enough gear for a week."

We spent the next hour discussing where the radio post should be built, and how much information I could give to Aunt Rosie and the Manigaults. After Grandfather felt confident I knew what to do, I went upstairs to pack my bag.

I had just crawled into bed when the old man tapped on the door.

"I came up to apologize to you. I took it for granted that you would want to help with the coast watch, but I should have asked how you felt about it. I'm sorry."

"Don't worry," I said. "I'm just glad that you're giving me

something important to do. And you don't have to worry about me spilling the beans."

"I know that. I wanted you to know that your feelings are important to me, and you are not like some hired hand to be ordered around."

I noticed how tired my grandfather looked. I doubted he had slept three hours in the last three days. His eyes drooped and his haggard expression showed plainly that he was skating on the edge of exhaustion.

"I know, Grandfather. We'll get the radio system up and find Gaspar's killer too. But you need to get some sleep. We have miles to go and people to see tomorrow."

He got up, yawning. "I guess you're right. Good night, Harley."

7

A Cry in the Night

Grandfather rowed me across from the mainland dock using a boat the Manigault family always left for visitors. The sun, only two hours high in the sky, had already burned away the morning chill and fog. The day promised to be a scorcher.

I leaned over the side of the craft watching schools of mullet darting and flashing just below the surface through a glassy, blue-green sea. Far below the churning swarm of baitfish I could see the dark shadows of tarpons and barracudas, ever present, ever hungry, and ever dangerous.

I thought Bear Paw would be one of those sand and palm tree keys that you see in magazines. It wasn't. In some distant age, the sea had cut a deep channel, a mile wide, leaving several hundred acres of prime woodland separated from the rest of Timucua County. Looking at a map, it looked like some monstrous bear had left a footprint in the Gulf as it fled north through Wildcat Bay.

Grandfather repeated my instructions on the trip from the ranch to the Manigault's wharf. Norman Manigault and I were to prepare a building for the radio as quickly as possible. I would then monitor the radio on the island until I received messages from the ranch, Ortiz Point, and Ollis' Sawmill before returning to the mainland. Once we completed the network, I would help direct operations from the ranch.

We headed for the south end, or heel, of the island. The old man rowed easily and smoothly for a landlubber.

Aunt Rosie and Beth lived in a rambling Victorian mansion, built for Rosie by Commodore Manigault. The two women met us at the wharf. I couldn't help smiling at the sight of Beth standing barefoot on the dock in a pair of faded overalls. I had thought about her often since the day of my father's memorial, and I hoped we could spend some time together while I visited the island.

"Beth saw you coming almost before you left the mainland dock," Aunt Rosie explained. "I told you, that girl has eyes like a hawk."

"Beth," Grandfather called before we even docked "would you run up to Norman's place and ask him to come down here if he has time?"

The girl took off running, fleet and nimble as a young deer.

I lugged my valise up to the house, and Aunt Rosie told me to sit in the parlor while she and Grandfather went to the kitchen to catch up on the news and brew a fresh pot of coffee. I hoped she might also find some cookies or rolls. Grandfather and I had left the ranch before daylight with nothing but leftover biscuits, drizzled with cane syrup, for breakfast.

The parlor reminded me of a tight-fitting pair of shoes—pretty but terribly uncomfortable. The old-fashioned furniture, narrow and stuffed with horsehair, must have been designed for skinny women wearing bustles. One thing seemed certain—the designers of the couches and chairs never had men or boys in mind when they created those monstrosities.

A life-sized portrait of Commodore Boaz Manigault dominated the room. The legendary Confederate blockade-runner had been as rich as King Midas. He had owned a fleet of three ships that hauled cattle from Peru Landing and Tampa to Cuba, and returned bearing chests of Spanish gold. The old seaman must have been in his mid-sixties, and twice a widower, when he married Rosie Wallace. She was twenty and pregnant with Uncle Norman when a drunken cattle buyer killed him in Havana.

I have heard a whispered family legend that Aunt Rosie sent a member of the Wallace family—likely my grandfather—to Cuba to ensure that the killer received justice. He discovered that local officials had only put the grandee under house arrest, which must have struck Grandfather as an insufficient punishment for killing his sister's husband. A day or two later, Cuban police found the killer hanging from a rafter in his villa overlooking Havana harbor. With a sigh of relief, they closed the book on the whole affair, declaring it a suicide.

The portrait artist had captured the old commodore for posterity with one hand on the wheel of the ship and the other pointing at some unseen sailor. A touch of insanity glittered in those dark eyes, and I figured that few visitors ever stayed long with that old rogue scowling down at them from his perch on the wall.

When Norman and Beth returned, Aunt Rosie called me into the kitchen. I helped myself to a second breakfast of coffee and fried doughnuts covered with powdered sugar while Grandfather Wallace explained our mission.

"Don't worry, Perry," Norman reassured Grandfather. "We'll have everything ready for the sailors by the end of the day. Harley can stay and monitor radio traffic until the other three stations are in operation, and then I'll have Beth sail him over to the ranch."

The promise seemed to take a weight from my grandfather's shoulders, but I was confused.

"Aren't you going to be here?" I asked.

"I've contracted with the pencil company in Cedar Key to haul a load of supplies to a work crew up on the mouth of Rattlesnake Run. I planned on leaving this afternoon, but with a full moon, I can sail tonight, load up in Cedar Key, and deliver the food and liquor by tomorrow noon."

Grandfather gulped down a cup of steaming coffee, kissed Aunt Rosie's cheek, and got ready to leave. "Sorry to inconvenience you," he said to Norman. "I know I can count on you and Harley. I'm sending Stumpy up to the sawmill, and John and I are going to Ortiz Point. Time is fleeting."

"You be careful around Ortiz," Norman warned Grandfather as he was getting back into the boat. "Remember what happened to Gaspar down there."

A black look of murderous anger flashed across Grandfather's scarred face. "I haven't forgotten that for a minute," he hissed. "You can bet your boats and everything you hold dear on that."

Without a further word he pushed off, pulling on the oars with easy strokes.

Norman and Florry lived on the northern end of Bear Paw Island, his house on the lee side of a hill. Florry came outside, waved, and went about her tasks. Beth told me later that Florry kept herself busy all the time to keep from worrying herself sick about her two grown sons who had joined the Marines the day after Pearl Harbor.

"We might as well use that old smokehouse," Norman grunted, striding toward a ramshackle hut perched on the brow of a high dune about three hundred yards from the Gulf. "No need to reinvent the wheel."

I could have thought of a better cliché, but his point made perfect sense. Why should we build a radio shack when we already had an empty building?

The cabin was a simple, one-room log structure. It sagged

a little and some of the chinking had fallen from between the logs, but I suspected it would take a direct hit from a major hurricane to make the smokehouse even shiver.

Norman and I worked hard all day getting the little shack in shape. We put on a new tin roof, chinked the walls with cement, and put a window in the wall facing the Gulf. "This may seem like a lot of extra work," Norman said, as we sweated to cut an opening for the window, "but whoever mans this station next will appreciate a cross-breeze when the hot days come."

While we worked, Beth and Florry grabbed mops, brooms, and a pail of sudsy water, and began to clean away twenty-five years of filth and smoke. Not content to simply scrub the room, they hung curtains, installed a cot with a colorful quilt, and brought a bookcase up from the house full of Western novels and outdoor magazines.

Norman put the final touch on the radio shack. He tacked up a government topographical map on the wall above the table. The blue of the Gulf and the green of western Timucua County split the map almost in half. The dark blue, indicating the deep channels, stood out in stark contrast to the pale blue of the shallows. The dark greens, denoting the vast, unbroken forests of the Wildcat Bay region, covered the land area, unbroken except for the light blue of the creeks and rivers. A few black dots showed the location of the county's scattered ranches and homesteads. I couldn't take my eyes off that chart.

I spent the night in the converted smokehouse, looking at the map and reading until I fell asleep. Norman left on his supply run to Rattlesnake Run as soon as the moon rose above the trees.

Beth came early the next morning, and we ate breakfast with Florry. The two talked incessantly, but I blanked out the girl talk. I had other things on my mind.

We'd been awake for hours when the small naval vessel tied up at Norman's dock. The ship could easily have been mistaken for a rich tycoon's cabin cruiser except for the steel gray paint and a Y-shaped hoist on the stern.

A crew of surly sailors unloaded several heavy boxes marked "fragile." They staggered up the hill with their burden, grumbling all the way. They cheered up considerably when Florry invited them to the house for a late breakfast.

Beth and I stayed in the converted smokehouse watching a thin yeoman named Hiram Wyckham put the radio unit together. The communications specialist explained in some detail how to use the large batteries without draining them of too much power. When he had the system installed, he allowed Beth and me to turn on the receiver and flip the dials and listen to the radio traffic. He left the radio shack as soon as possible, hurrying down to the house where the smell of coffee and frying bacon wafted on the sea breeze.

The amount of chatter coming from the radio amazed us. Most of the messages were from transport ships lumbering through the Gulf heading toward New Orleans, Mobile, and Galveston. Beth and I spent the day listening to the radio and chatting about what we heard. She sure was easy to talk to.

We laughed at the tongue-in-cheek monologue of a sheriff in the panhandle alerting officers in the surrounding jurisdictions that a kid had stolen a superior judge's Mercury. They believed the boy planned to drive to Pensacola to enlist in the Navy. The judge suggested tying the young thief to the rear bumper of the car and making him run behind the Mercury all the way home. But whatever else happened, the judge ordered, the officers must not hurt his automobile. A Santa Rosa County deputy broke in a few minutes later to report that he had recovered the car and put the patriotic young thief on the bus to Pensacola.

North of Tampa, the captain of a Cuban freighter

reported spotting a German U-boat lurking near the coast. I thought this revelation might cause an uproar, but only stony silence greeted the message. Beth and I decided that because of the seaman's broken English, no one was taking the message seriously.

No sound issued from our coast watch channel except an occasional burst of static.

"I guess I better be going home," Beth finally said.

"Do you really have to go?" I asked, and found myself blushing.

She looked at me in the strangest way, then shrugged her shoulders. "If I don't, Aunt Rosie will come looking for me."

I nodded okay, but I really hated to see her go. She smelled nice (like my real mother), and she made me smile. But mostly I would miss Beth because she understood me as no adult ever could. I could tell her things I would never share with my grandfather, Norman, or even Brother Stumpy.

"Are you coming back tomorrow?" I asked.

"Of course, silly. Aunt Florry will spend most of the day with Aunt Rosie tomorrow. They get lonely with Uncle Norman and the boys gone. We can probably spend the whole day together, and by suppertime, they will have fixed a meal fit for a king."

I walked her outside. A bright orange sun hovered just above the Gulf's horizon line. The forest would be completely dark in an hour. A nearby covey of quail, scattered by some unseen predator, began whistling their plaintive "bob-bob-white" call to gather the flock. By instinct they sensed that they were vulnerable alone. I knew how they felt.

Beth brushed my arm lightly, gave me a big smile, and skipped off down the path.

A gloom seemed to settle over the little room with Beth gone. I ate supper with Florry and then went back to the cabin and read for a while by the light of a kerosene lamp. I fiddled a little with the radio, but mostly just left it on the wavelength General Bullard had assigned to our coast watch unit. Without Beth to joke with, eavesdropping on the other channels was no fun.

I left the window and door open to allow the sea breezes to cool the room, but the light from the kerosene lamp flickered and sputtered in the wind. Strange shadows played tag along the walls. I carefully studied the map Norman had tacked to the wall, trying to acquaint myself with the region.

Half-asleep, I was struggling to finish an article about hunting for moose in Canada, when the call came in. There was a roar of static followed almost immediately by a strangled cry: "Danger! We need help! Ortiz . . . " Then the radio went dead.

I recognized the voice immediately. John, Grandfather's loyal cowhand and friend, had screamed the warning. I sat and listened for a few minutes, but nothing but silence and a feeling of loss and dread filled the room.

John would never have broadcast a call for help unless he and my grandfather had serious problems. I decided to contact General Bullard, report the call, and ask for orders.

I had tacked a copy of the call sign the general had given Grandfather to report emergencies on the wall beside the radio. I found the right wavelength and clicked the squawk box to transmit.

"This is the Timucua County Coast Watch unit and I have a message for General Bullard."

Nothing happened. No sound followed, except the echo of my voice in the little room.

I tried again, with no better luck. I got out the military manual and reviewed the procedures. I checked the connection wires and battery. The receiver worked, loud and clear. Just to be certain that I had not made a mistake, I followed the transmission schedule step-by-step. The transmitter sat on the table, silent and lifeless as a rock. I silently cursed Hiram Wyckham for being more concerned about filling his belly than getting his job done correctly.

What should I do next? I took a deep breath and tried to think. I could try to use Mr. Levy's telephone, but I did not have Bullard's number, and little hope of ever prying it from the security-conscious military. I could spend two or three days trying to organize a posse from the old and crippled men of the county. But by the time I could collect fifteen men able to ride, Grandfather Wallace and John would probably be dead.

I tried the transmitter one last time, but I might just as well have been screaming into the mouth of the Sphinx.

There comes a time in every person's life when they make one decision that changes all other aspects of their life. Some people agonize over that choice or try to peer into the future to see the possible consequences of their decision. I did neither. I simply reached the conclusion that Grandfather and John were in trouble, and if anyone was going to save them, it would have to be me. Had I been smarter or more sophisticated, I would have looked for a softer choice—one that allowed me to keep out of danger but still look at myself in the mirror. But no one ever accused me of being sophisticated.

I took five minutes to jot a note explaining what had happened. I folded the topo map of the coastline, put it under my belt, and closed the door to the radio post on Bear Paw Island for the last time.

The path from Norman's house to Rosie's mansion had been worn smooth and hard by a thousand feet on hundreds of errands. Where a tidal creek turned the trail into mud, someone had constructed a simple wooden bridge. Sections of the footpath ran under tall pines and a heavy canopy of oak, but even in the darkest section of the forest, enough moonlight filtered through the leaves to light the way.

Rosie left the front door of her house unlocked, as did

most country folk. I slipped down the back hallway, past the glowering gaze of Commodore Manigault, and found the door to Beth's bedroom. It creaked a little when I pushed it open. I froze for a minute, but heard no sound from Rosie's room. Beth's soft, even breathing told me that the sound had not disturbed the girl.

She looked beautiful. Bathed in the glow of moonlight, her hair shone like spun gold and her face was as serene as a painting of an angel.

I clamped my hand over her mouth, and her eyes flew open. I saw a brief look of fear. I started to whisper for her to be quiet but never got the chance. She seemed to relax for a second and then rolled forward and smashed her knee into the side of my face. The swift, hard blow knocked me against the wall, and pain exploded in my temple and bright lights flashed before my eyes.

Before I could recover my senses, she rolled off the bed and landed atop me, her knees crashing into my stomach. That sudden attack knocked the wind out of me, and as I struggled to catch my breath, she began clawing at my face with her fingernails.

"Beth, stop!" I finally managed to yell. "It's me—Harley."

She stopped scratching me, but glared at me with angry, suspicious eyes. She did not take her knees up, but continued to pin my arms to the floor.

"What are you doing here? I thought you were a … an intruder."

"Let me up. Grandfather and John are in trouble. I need you to sail me over to the ranch."

"What do you mean in trouble?"

"I'll explain on the way, but we need to hurry."

Beth got up and sat on the edge of the bed. My face hurt but not nearly as much as my pride.

I noticed for the first time that Rosie had not appeared,

though we had made enough noise to awaken a good-sized cemetery. I backed over into a corner, away from the door, figuring that I'd very soon see the barrel of a shotgun poking around the corner.

"Is Rosie out?" I whispered.

"No. She is almost stone deaf without her hearing aids. A train could run through the parlor at night and she'd never know it."

I began to relax. Beth stood watching me for a minute and then said, "I thought you were in a hurry."

"I am. We need to go."

"Well, I can't get dressed with you standing there. Why don't you grab us some food from the kitchen, and I'll be out in five minutes."

8

To Die in the Wilderness

Beth handled the tiller skillfully, and we ran through choppy little waves, pushed by a strong northwest breeze. I had never been out of sight of land before. I felt a little seasick and my face hurt like fury. This had certainly been a humiliating night. Since midnight, Beth had knocked me down and pinned me there, scratched my face, and now I felt sure that I was about to further embarrass myself by vomiting all over the deck of her boat.

The little vessel was her pride and joy. Norman had built it for her as a gift for her thirteenth birthday. It measured sixteen feet in length and was very light and maneuverable. The boat had a single sail, which in sailing jargon, I'd been told, made it a catboat. Norman had painted it red at the bottom, white at the top, and had named it the *Bonnie Beth*.

I lay with my back to the mast, sick and licking my wounds. The girl sat in the stern, manning the rudder. I concentrated on keeping my head down, a head that had already been knocked twice, first by Beth's knee, then by the boom of this little boat. I am sometimes a slow learner, but getting hit in the head by the swing of the boom convinced me of the need to keep my head down. Beth pretended not to see the accident, but I could not help noticing that she shook her head in pity in the darkness.

"How do you know that Uncle Perry is in trouble?" Beth asked, breaking the long silence.

I told her about the call for help on the radio and my futile attempt to get in touch with General Bullard.

"So what are you going to do at the ranch?" she queried.

"I'm going to get horses and head down to Ortiz Point and find out what's wrong."

"Are you crazy? It's too dangerous."

"What do you suggest, Miss Smarty Pants? Leave Grandfather and John down there without help?"

"We need to get some help from adults," she said, after thinking the problem over for a couple of minutes. "We could gather up a posse and go down there in force."

I ignored the "we" in her last sentence, but I also saw the problem with her plan. Due to the war, there were only twenty-five to thirty people left at Peru Landing, almost all of them old, crippled, or women. There were still a few cowmen in Timucua County, too old for the military but able to ride hard and shoot, but they were scattered on ranches over an area of a hundred miles.

"How long do you think it would take to get together fifteen or twenty adults who could fight? I'm not willing to wait that long."

She didn't respond to that. Typical of a girl, I thought. They never admit they're wrong.

Leaving the pale, moonlit waters of the Gulf, we entered the Wildcat an hour before first light. Beth worked hard to make the *Bonnie Beth* creep forward against the river current, and she said nothing for a while. A single light, at Mr. Levy's Mercantile, indicated the presence of Peru Landing on the opposite shore, but we did not stop. Even Beth realized that the town offered no help for our problem.

A river at night is completely different from the same stretch of water in the daylight. Only slivers of moonlight seeped through the leaves, and predators prowled close to the surface in the inky darkness. My eyes soon adjusted to the gloom, but there was little to see. Splashes and thunks gave proof that Nature's nightly dance of death continued just below the surface in the pre-dawn stillness.

The trip up the Wildcat seemed to take forever. We finally tied Beth's boat to the tiny wharf down the hill from Grandfather's ranch house a few minutes before first light.

Five or six horses stamped impatiently in the corral as we hurried up to the ranch. I stopped and caught two, tying them to the posts and letting the others loose. The freed animals went a few feet from the log enclosure and began cropping the lush grass. I had no idea how long my trip would take, or whether I would even return alive, and there was no reason to leave the poor creatures cooped up in the corral.

I hurried to the barn and brought the two tethered horses a couple of scoops of corn. While they ate, I brought out two saddles and bridles. I figured I'd need a horse for Grandfather, one way or another. I just hoped he'd be riding it back. The horses ignored the implements of work and munched contentedly on the grain.

Beth sat on the front porch, waiting. When I went up to the house, she was ready.

"I don't like this plan of yours," she said, the worry showing on her face.

"Yeah, I know," I replied. "You've made that abundantly clear."

"I know that Uncle Perry wouldn't want you to do anything that might get you hurt."

"Well, that is about rule number twenty. Rule number one is that you never abandon a family member or friend who is in trouble."

She nodded slowly but said nothing. Beth followed me into the house. She wanted to continue the argument, but she knew the Wallace code. Her concern touched me, but I knew what had to be done, and she did too.

To change the subject, I asked, "Have you ever been to Ortiz Point?"

"I've sailed down to the Point a couple of times. I've never gone there overland."

I pulled out the coastal map and spread it on the dining table. We both leaned over, looking at the lines and colors. An unbroken swath of green indicated forests and swamps stretching from the Wildcat to the southwestern county line. The obvious route—the way I would have taken under normal circumstances—led south past the ranch till it intersected with the road leading from Ortiz Point to Pigbone. But these were far from normal times.

"Beth," I finally said. "Look only at the Point. Does this look like you remember it?"

She took a stubby pencil, placing four little dots on the point of land, which jutted into the Gulf like a fishhook with a goiter. While she worked with the pencil, she gave me a brief history lesson of Ortiz Point.

"Aunt Rosie says Rueben Ortiz lived like a hermit. She thought he might have been a mixed blood—half-Spanish and half-Seminole. He was too old to be conscripted during the War Between the States, but he piloted the commodore's blockade-runner because no one knew the coastline as well as he did. During the cattle boom, he made a fortune in Cuban gold captaining one of the commodore's ships, but he lived by himself in a fishing shack. Aunt Rosie figured he buried a fortune at the Point, but I don't guess anyone ever found it."

"Do you think that's what this mystery is—treasure hunters?"

She shook her head, and then shrugged her shoulders. "Who knows? It could be anything."

"What are those dots you put on the map?"

"When I was last there, there were three or four ramshackle fishing huts. Might have been headquarters for a group of rich fishermen who used to come down here before the Depression."

I took the map, folded it up, and stuck it behind my back in the waistband of my pants. Too much time had already been wasted. Whatever trouble Grandfather and John had encountered, piddling around the ranch would not help them.

I went upstairs and put on my father's broad-brimmed hat and found a blanket. Rolling up a change of clothes in the quilt, I took down his saddlebags. I don't know why, but carrying a piece of my father's life with me on this expedition gave me some comfort.

From the gun cabinet I took Grandfather's 1903 Springfield and several boxes of cartridges. For personal protection I took my father's little .32 pistol, a box of bullets, and a pump shotgun.

At the door, Beth handed me a canteen of fresh water and a paper sack of food. Worry lines were etched on her face, but she did not try to stop me.

"Be careful," she said, holding my hand for a second.

"I will," I promised. "Are you going back to Bear Paw or are you going to stay here?"

"I'm going to try and find some men who will come help you."

"I left a note for Florry and Aunt Rosie, but you might stop by the Landing and see if Mr. Levy will try to call General Bullard."

I put my saddle on a little bay horse I had ridden several times, and hitched Grandfather's saddle on his big chestnut stud, tethering him to the saddle horn using a short length of rope. I put the guns and blanket roll on the chestnut and mounted.

"I'm going to take the road as far south as Widow Woman Slough," I told her, "then I'm going to cut through the swamps. Gaspar followed the road, and so must Grandfather and John, since the truck is gone."

She nodded in agreement. "You'll lose some time, but it's safer."

Feeling bold and confident for a change, I leaned forward to kiss her cheek. She turned her face quickly and our lips met for a second. I felt a thrill and excitement unlike anything I had ever felt before.

I whipped off my hat, gave her a small grin, and then put my heels to the little bay. He jumped once, then lined out at a fast gallop down the trail. The chestnut loped along easily beside us.

Once we left the ranch, the forest immediately swallowed us up. The two-rut road and widely spaced fences were the only signs of civilization in the virgin woodlands. Pines, straight and tall, grew on the sand hills, and oak and clumps of cypress grew in dense clusters in the wet bottomlands. Palmetto and dog fennels grew among the pines, while thick brush and brambles made the lowland forest virtually impenetrable.

I didn't know exactly how far it was to Ortiz Point, but I figured it at about fifteen to eighteen miles. By my reckoning, I figured I should be safe until I reached Widow Woman Slough. Brother Stumpy and John had backtracked Gaspar's horse to there without finding any trace of trouble. From the map, the slough looked to be a little more than halfway to the Ortiz Point at Pigbone Road.

Two hours into my journey, I spied a small, spring-fed pond, and decided to rest the horses and try to locate my position on the map. In cowboy movies, the good guy can run his horse at a full gallop across a hundred miles of desert without the horse or rider breaking a lather. Real men and horses are not as tough as these Hollywood heroes. We mere mortals get tired and sweaty, and sitting astride a horse for long stretches makes ordinary humans stiff and sore.

While the animals noisily slurped water, I rummaged

through the saddlebags for the sack of food Beth had packed. Her idea of a hearty lunch proved disappointing. She must have packed for a girl trying to lose weight. The paper bag included only a small can of peaches, two leftover biscuits, and a small slice of salty Virginia ham.

I managed to open the can of peaches with my pocketknife without cutting my hand. I ate the fruit, drank the sugary syrup, and polished off the rest of the food, except for a single biscuit, relying on the old adage of the Rebel soldiers that food is carried better in your stomach than on your back. I buried the can, to keep some poor coon or possum from winding up wearing a tin necklace.

The horses sensed the danger first. Their heads jerked up, looking back along the trail behind me, stamping nervously. It took me longer to make out the sound. At first, I would have sworn that a distant drummer was fast approaching my position. It took me a few seconds to recognize the racket as the hoof beats of a horse being ridden hard.

A dense thicket of wild grape vines and persimmon bushes located near a bend in the trail seemed to be the perfect place for an ambush. I squeezed into the thicket and squatted down. An opening in the leaves allowed me to see the road for several feet before the horseman reached my position. It all seemed perfect. I took out my father's .32 and waited, trying to control the shaking of my hand.

It finally dawned on me that my quest to find Grandfather was not a game but a dangerous and deadly serious operation. If I stumbled or hesitated in the wrong situation, I could wind up dead. Fear seized me like a clammy hand. I wondered if Grandfather would be ashamed of me. He always seemed so cold and efficient in action, with the medals and scars to prove it. I, on the other hand, felt my body trembling, and my brain seemed to scream: run, run, run!

The sound, now loud and steady, froze me in place. All I

saw from my hiding place was the blurry image of a galloping horse with a rider in a large hat leaning low across the animal's neck.

I dove into the road and sprang to my feet, screeching and waving my hat and gun wildly. I had planned to land a few feet in front of the horse and cause it to rear up. My timing was bad, and I wound up rolling almost under the creature's front feet. The horse's hooves whizzed past my head, narrowly missing taking off my right ear. I escaped by scrambling on all fours under the horse's belly.

The rider, who had managed to stay on the horse during its initial gyrations, rolled off the frightened animal, landing at my feet. The stunned rider lay face down on the trail. I slapped the small figure hard with my hat, and thumbed back the hammer of my pistol.

"Don't shoot! Don't shoot!" the rider screamed, rolling over and throwing up her hands for protection.

"Beth! What're you doing here"!

"I was coming to help you," she whispered, sobbing. Her body shook convulsively, her face streaked with dirt and tears.

"Beth, are you insane?" I howled. "This is not a game! I almost killed you." I couldn't help it. I screeched like a banshee, totally out of control.

"I noticed that," she said sniffing. "You are a lot like Uncle Perry. 'Death's firstborn.' That's what they call him behind his back. It's a Bible quote, I think. It means . . ."

I put my hand over her mouth again. She was babbling to cover her jittery nerves, I knew. She got an angry look in her eyes, but this time she did not kick me. I realized later I should have hugged her, but I felt so frightened and high-strung, I could not think straight. When she finally settled down, I took my hand off her mouth.

"Now, what are you doing here?" I asked.

"I came to help you. I know where we can get some adults

who will help. I've been riding hard to try to catch you before you left the road."

"Oh, I thought you were just trying to kill that horse," I said, hoping she would hear the sarcastic tone. "Now, where are you going to get this army?"

"Well, aren't you just so witty? If it weren't for Uncle Perry, I'd leave you out here to learn that you aren't so smart."

"I'm sorry, Beth. You about scared the bejubers out of me."

"Well, what do you think about me? I heard you cocking that pistol. You were going to shoot me, weren't you?"

I didn't reply, but we both knew the answer.

Beth's horse had run down the road when she fell off him, but now he came back to the little pond lured by the scent of other horses and fresh water. Beth went down to the little waterhole and washed her face. When she came back, I took out the stained and battered map.

We finally located the little spring-fed pond, a tiny dot of light blue near a bend in the trail, on the map. Widow Woman Slough was less than a mile to the southeast. The map revealed a swamp bordering a narrow inlet that fingered its way inland from the Gulf. Cutting through the marshland would cut many miles from the trip, but I suspected that whatever time I would save in distance would be lost due to terrain.

"When we get to the inlet," I said, pointing it out on the map, "I got to take to the swamps. Where are you going?" I ran my finger along the route I planned to take.

"I'll turn then and ride through the piney woods to Pigbone," Beth said.

"John told me to stay away from there. He said the only reason for a white boy to go there was to drink or look for . . . Do you think it's safe?"

"Dr. Tuskegee Pettigrew has bandaged your grandfather more times than either one of them can count. I'll go to his office. He won't let anything happen to a Wallace or Manigault kinsman."

I thought about it for a few moments and I knew she was right.

Gaspar had told me that a Union captain named Perigeone had established a colony for freedmen after the War Between the States on the banks of Lake Seminole. The town had been named for its founder but later corrupted into Pigbone. With a population of almost two hundred, it would still have a few men capable of firing guns, if they would come. It was Grandfather's best hope and mine. But it sure seemed a slim straw to rest our hopes on.

"I don't much like this, Beth. It's too dangerous."

"I know, but like you said, Uncle Perry's life may hang in the balance. I'll be careful. Besides, what else can we do?"

We caught the horses and rode in silence until we reached the slough. I was torn between worry about Beth and worry about my grandfather. The girl seemed unconcerned. She rode easily without a saddle or blanket, giving me that shy grin every time our eyes made contact.

"I'm sorry," I said when we finally reached the inlet that fed Widow Woman Slough.

"For what?" she asked.

"For what? For almost killing you, for scaring you last night, for screaming at you like a dog, for not trusting you? I'm sorry about everything."

"Don't worry. I'll meet you late this afternoon somewhere on the Ortiz Point Road," she said, and turning her horse, rode off through the piney woods toward Pigbone. I suddenly wanted to ride after her and kiss Beth. I wanted to tell the girl to come with me or beg her to go back to the ranch. I wanted . . . I didn't know what to do, but I sure hated to see her go.

Almost anything that a human considers uncomfortable or unhealthy, except frostbite, you will find in a swamp. On my four-mile slog through the marshlands I encountered alligators, snakes, mosquitoes, sand gnats, chiggers, briars, sawgrass, stagnant water, mud, and quicksand. Within a couple of hundred feet of leaving the trail, the horses and I were covered with mud.

The little bay horse and Grandfather's big chestnut proved virtually useless in swampy conditions. Most of the time, I led the frightened creatures. On one small hammock I found the prints of a panther, and the poor animals nearly went berserk at the scent of their ancient enemy. Only when we had left that clump of trees and dry ground far behind did the horses finally begin to act less skittish.

Twice I blundered out to the thin strip of sandy beaches bordering the Gulf. Each time I quickly faded back into the swamps, for whoever had caused trouble for my Grandfather would almost surely be watching the approaches to Ortiz Point from the Gulf.

The first sign that we were nearing the end of our journey came from the chestnut horse. He suddenly moved out in front, nostrils flared wide, and began leading us toward the southwest. At first I wondered if the animal had smelled the panther again, but it did not seem jittery or afraid. Then I realized that it had scented something familiar. That could only be other horses—that meant Grandfather, or John.

I tied the horses securely to a small cypress tree and slid the shotgun from the pack behind my saddle. Crouching low, I began slipping forward from tree to tree trying hard to make as little noise as possible. Every bush that rattled as I passed or every time my feet suctioned out of the mud sounded as loud as a gunshot in the still, quiet forest. Successful hunters soon learn the tricks for quiet movement in the woods, but my field experience was limited to a few squirrel hunts with my father.

I saw openings in the trees ahead, indicating that the Gulf

was nearby. I slid to the ground and crawled forward. I found John first. He was obviously dead. His hands tied behind his back, he had already begun to bloat in the humid, fecund air. Tears began, and I could not stop them.

A few feet away, lay my grandfather. He too had his hands tied, and he lay still in a pool of blood.

9

Fight the Good Fight

Grandfather looked so strange lying beside a pile of discarded tin cans. He resembled a badly maimed cowboy doll some careless child had mistreated and abandoned. I looked from the bushes, but could find no sign of life. His thin, scarred face looked pale and drawn, like a corpse completely drained of blood.

I slithered over the muddy terrain to where he lay and put my finger on his wrist to check for a pulse. His eyes snapped open, trying to focus through the matted blood, flashing with a mixture of anger and surprise. I clamped my hand over his mouth to keep him from crying out, and he bit a large hunk of meat from the palm. I almost screamed out loud. Tears rolled down my cheeks, making rivulets of mud on my dirty face. I finally decided that putting my hand over a person's mouth was not the smart way to announce my arrival.

My hand hurt so badly that I had to use my teeth and uninjured hand to open my pocketknife. Leaning close to his ear I whispered, "If I cut the ropes, can you move?"

"I think so," he grunted. "We got to try."

Grandfather Wallace was barely able to wobble to his feet. He leaned heavily on me, and I managed to get him back to the little clearing where I had left the horses. I examined him, and he seemed barely alive.

Panting from the exertion of the short trip, he finally managed to gasp, "No need to go any further."

A little blood trickled down out of the corner of his mouth, and a coughing spasm revealed teeth and gums covered by a bright, gory froth. "The Germans hate the swamp. . . . Think I'm dead anyway."

"You mean the *Germans* did this?" I managed to whisper.

He nodded and lay with his back against a cypress tree. I gave him the canteen and after rummaging through my saddlebags found the stale biscuit I had saved. The old man ate and drank greedily, downing half of the canteen. While he devoured those scant rations, I opened his shirt to inspect his wound.

One look told the story. The bullet had hit him in the side, shattering a rib. Rather than plowing through his vitals, the bullet followed the curve of the bone, exiting through the skin in his upper chest. The injury seemed typical of Grandfather's life. His survival always seemed to be bought with suffering and grief.

I opened my blanket roll and tore my clean shirt into wide strips. I poured some water from the canteen to cleanse his wounds and bandaged him tightly. He grunted a time or two when I pulled the cotton material tight but said nothing. I took the leftover cloth to bind my bleeding hand.

"Looks like you were lucky," I said. "That rib bone has got to hurt like Hades, and you're weak from loss of blood, but you should be safe to travel."

"Can't go," he muttered shaking his head.

"We've got to. We need to get you to a doctor, and get the army in here to clean out this murdering scum."

"Can't leave."

"Why not?"

It took Grandfather almost ten minutes, stopping often to catch his breath or wait for a spasm of pain to pass, but he finally managed to tell the story.

He and John had driven to the Point and put the radio in working order, using the old hermit's shack as a base of operations. A squad of twelve or fourteen German commandos must have paddled ashore from a submarine after dark, and they surprised the two cowmen. John had been killed immediately, yelling his warning into the transmitter. Grandfather lasted a little longer by playing dumb.

"I didn't let on that I spoke a little German," he muttered with a bloody grin. "They've had an agent in the area for a couple of weeks. He has located the air base and decided on Ortiz Point as a secluded place from which to carry out a raid. I think the agent was the one who killed Gaspar."

"How did you get shot?" I asked.

"It was supposed to be an execution. They questioned me a little in English, and I told them I was a simple cowman who had been hired to man the radio. When they thought they had all the information I knew, they tied my hands, took me into the woods, and shot me. The German gunman didn't even check to see if I was dead. Just left me like a road-killed possum."

The old man took another sip of water and rested for a minute before finishing his story.

"My German is a little rusty, but I learned they plan to destroy the airbase. They'll leave tonight, right after dark, and they have to be back before daybreak for the U-boat to pick them up. That's why we can't leave."

"You're hurt," I countered, "and I don't think I can stand up to a trained squad of German killers by myself."

"You're looking at this all wrong," he said. "We've got them bottled up. There's maybe two hours till dark. They'll stay indoors till then. They hate going into the swamp, and the only ways out are the sea and along the main road. We've got to keep the cork in the bottle until help arrives."

"Beth's gone to see a doctor in Pigbone to get help."

"Tuskegee Pettigrew?"

I nodded. "Will they help?"

"I reckon so. If they can get organized in time."

The old man rested another minute, his eyes closed as if in prayer. "Sometimes we have to do things we would rather not do," he said quietly. "It seems to be the natural order of life. I promised the souls of your mother and father that I would be a good grandfather to you, and that you would never have blood on your hands because of me. Now it seems I've got to break that promise."

"I'll do my best," I said, though my knees were already beginning to shake. I worried that I would fail him. Grandfather might forgive me of any other sin, but he would never respect a coward.

Grandfather outlined his plans in a few words. He was going to move to the road with his Springfield rifle to cork the bottle. My job was to slip in close to the clearing at Ortiz Point and open up with the scattergun to addle the Germans. I had seventeen shells. Once I had fired them, he ordered me to slip back to my horse and head back to the road junction to direct the reinforcements from Pigbone.

"You got buckshot," the old man said, "but I doubt it'll do much more than sting anyone it hits from the range you'll be shooting." He closed his eyes, as if to block out an image he was unwilling to view. "Remember: whatever you do, never fire more than three shots from any one position. Your job is not to kill but to confuse."

A few raindrops fell and then stopped as quickly as they started. In all the excitement, I had failed to notice how dark the sky in the west had become. I had no doubt that in half an hour we would be fighting in a downpour.

With a plan in place, Grandfather seemed reenergized. He managed to pull himself into the saddle of the big chestnut, but the strain came with a price. A new trickle of blood blossomed on the white bandage.

I reached up to steady the old man in the saddle. He took my hand and gasped. "If you have any hint of danger—any hint, at all—you get out of here. Leave. Fade into the marsh and disappear. I'll find you later. I would never forgive myself if anything happened to you." He looked at my bandaged hand. "And sorry I bit you. I hope that's the worst that happens to you."

He turned once in the saddle and whispered, "Wait until you hear me whistle. Then open up with everything you've got."

He disappeared as quietly as a forest ghost, and I huddled near the clearing as a light rain began falling. A roll of thunder echoed out over the Gulf. The only sign of life at the Point was a man in a striped flannel shirt and suspenders who slipped out the backdoor of the shack to visit the outhouse. I knew it was a German and marveled that he looked pretty ordinary.

The wait for Grandfather's signal seemed to last for an eternity. I began to wonder if the old man had fallen or died. The mind plays tricks on you in times of stress. All the things you fear most flash into your brain. A couple of times I considered getting my horse and going to look for the old warrior. But something in my training or heritage made the thought of leaving my post inexcusable. I spent the time figuring where I'd run for each of my volleys.

Through the shroud of darkness, I thought a detected the soft whistle. I wondered if I had imagined the sound, but it was quickly repeated, louder and more confident the second time.

I aimed the shotgun at the door and fired three quick shots. From far off, the sharp crack of a rifle seemed to offer a ringing exclamation point to the end of my first volley.

I ran, slipping in the wet dirt, to a large sweetgum tree

that I had chosen as my second place to fire. From the cabin, a short burst of automatic weapon fire ripped through the thicket where I had been just a few moments before.

My grandfather's voice, strong and confident, rolled across the clearing, speaking in perfect German.

"Take this, you German pigs!"

I pulled the trigger of the shotgun, pumping off three more shots as quickly as my arm could move. Splinters flew from tough cypress siding along the whole Gulf side of the shack, and the lone window on that side of the house disintegrated in my hail of buckshot. I heard the commandos scrambling around inside the building, and someone yelled something in German that I took to be a curse.

Two quick shots from my grandfather's Springfield followed my shots, and I scurried to a small bank in a dry creek bed. A strong voice shouted a question through the window in German, but I could neither understand it nor cared what was being said. My fighting blood raged through me, quick and wild, like a Highland reel.

My grandfather's confident voice, again in German, replied with a pride that was obvious from the tone: *"You're in my country!"*

I saw the door cracking open. I realized one of the Germans must be trying for a shot at my last position, and I fired my next three shots at the small opening. It quickly slammed shut, but I barely noticed. I was already running for my next position.

My part in the battle of Ortiz Point felt like a thousand years, but really lasted less than twenty minutes. When the last shell ejected, in my battle madness, I felt as if the Winchester 12-gauge had somehow betrayed me. I dropped the weapon into the mud and reluctantly began making my way back toward my horse.

I didn't see the German until he stepped out of the bushes

as I was getting into the saddle. He held an ugly Luger pistol that every boy in America had already seen so often in the newsreels. His flannel shirt and suspenders betrayed him as the man who had slipped out to visit the outhouse. Caught outdoors when the storm of gunfire enveloped the little hut, he must have slipped around looking for the shooters.

Balancing on the stirrup, I came up with a plan spawned in a moment of desperation. I flipped over the horse, trying to keep the animal's body between me and the German. I attempted to draw my father's pistol while falling, but I hit the ground hard and the revolver flew from my hand. I lay stunned, gasping for air.

The German dove on me, grabbing me by the throat. I kicked at him, but there was little strength left in my legs. He jammed a knee into my chest and swung the Luger hard at the side of my head.

Everything went black.

10

Blood Moon Night

I awoke groggy and about as miserable as a human being can get.
My back and legs ached from the long ride, and my head hurt
so badly I wanted to rip it off and throw it into the Gulf. The
German had tied my hands behind my back. I flexed my wrists to
see if the ropes had any play in them. They did not. The cords bit
into the skin and seemed, if anything, to get tighter.

The roar of gunfire near the cabins seemed to be increasing.
The German jerked me to my feet and wiggled his pistol in the
direction of Rueben Ortiz's shack. He jabbed me in the back to
increase my speed and began jabbering at me in German. I didn't
understand a word he said, but soon figured out that *schnell* must
be the most frequently used word in his language.

I wondered what the German planned to do next. I imagined
it involved pushing me into the clearing and, using me as a
hostage, ordering Grandfather to either surrender or let them
pass. Knowing the old man, I doubted that he would ever do
either.

Out of the corner of my eye I saw a blur and heard a dull
thud. One second the German had been popping the muzzle of a
Luger in my back and the next he was stretched out on the
ground as unconscious as a brick.

A black man materialized from behind a live oak tree, carrying a heavy rifle by the barrel. He resembled a football player or

wrestler, well over six feet tall and heavily muscled. I guessed his age at about sixty, but I could not tell from his calm, unlined face.

"Howdy," he said, as casually as if we were two cowmen who had met riding fences and stopped to exchange gossip. "You must be Harley."

I nodded.

"Glad we got here in time. Your grandpa was beginning to get right testy. Figured maybe you found an apple pie and was hoggin' it all to yourself."

He laughed at his own joke and began cutting the ropes around my wrists. I reckoned that my reputation as a pie thief would follow me to the grave—which suddenly seemed a little farther off.

He stuck out a huge hand and said, "I'm Aaron Grant, but most folks just call me Big Aaron." He pointed to three black men standing in the shadows. "That's Willie, Jamie, and Jigsaw."

Willie and Jamie looked like old men. Jigsaw was only a year or two older than me, chubby and moon-faced. He wore clothes too fancy for a walk in the swamp, and I wondered if his momma had dressed him in his Sunday best for this trip. He tried to act nonchalant, but I noticed Jigsaw's fingers drumming incessantly on the stock of the 30-06 he carried. "If you're nervous now, wait until the bullets started flying past your ear," I thought, but only nodded a greeting.

"Big Aaron," I said, "if you've got another rifle, I can be of help."

"Thanks, but we'll just have to make do. Your grandpa wants you to join him over by the road. I think he is really worried about you."

Big Aaron hog-tied the German and led his little squad toward the clearing. I watched as he positioned his troops. Laughing, he whistled a few bars of "Over There" to calm his men. Jigsaw he placed behind a sand dune near the beach, putting the boy as far from danger as he could. The big man stationed Willie and Jamie behind thick trees around the clearing, and finally he crouched down opposite the door of the Ortiz shack. That impressed me. Putting himself in the most dangerous position showed both his skill as a leader and his courage.

I couldn't find the horse. The noise of battle had obviously spooked him. I searched the body of the unconscious German for my father's pistol and found nothing. I should have known that Big Aaron wouldn't have been that slipshod. I hunted around the cypress grove and finally located the gun under a clump of palmetto. The German must have kicked it there while I lay unconscious, considering it too small to worry about. I checked it carefully to make certain that the muzzle hadn't been plugged with mud.

It took me about fifteen minutes, slipping from tree to palmetto clump, from ditch to thicket, to reach Grandfather's position on the road. He looked terrible. Blood covered his shirt and face, and he seemed almost insane with battle fever. Something human seemed to replace the demonic rage when he saw me.

"Harley, I feared the worst when you didn't get back."

"A German had me, but Big Aaron almost took his head off with a gun butt."

"Good man. He fought with the Ninety-second Division Bolo boys during the Great War. They showed the Frenchies a thing or two about killing Germans."

Several black men and boys were stretched in a rough skirmish line around Grandfather's position. They had come from Pigbone with Big Aaron, who had taken Willie, Jamie, and Jigsaw to find me and provide some flanking fire. The rest of the men had stayed with Grandfather.

Beth was there too, and she acted like she was mad at the

whole world. Jamie told me later that Big Aaron had made the mistake of suggesting that she stay in town. She had pitched such a royal fit that the men had brought her along just to get her to calm down.

Night fell around us with seeming reluctance, as if some modern-day Joshua had stopped the sun in its course. Finally a shroud of darkness, wet and pitch black, signaled the return of the time for predators. The gunfire sputtered to a close with nightfall, and an eerie quiet finally settled over Ortiz Point. Even the tree frogs, generally oblivious to the presence of humans or too stupid to care, remained quiet.

What followed may have been one of the strangest councils of battle in the history of warfare. Seven black men—four of them old and three barely in their teens—joined Beth and me, squatting on the edge of a swamp in a ragged circle around Grandfather Wallace. Beth had not spoken to me since I came in, and her lips were drawn in a thin, tight line. Grandfather seemed to share her concerns. His shoulders drooped, and his haggard face wore a look of worry and exhaustion.

"Well, what do you think, Homer?" he finally asked.

An old man, barely visible in the darkness, pointed toward the bullet-riddled house. "I figure they're either gonna come chargin' down that road and try to bust through us, or slip out and head for the beach."

"Yeah," a second oldster muttered, "if they stayed out of the swamps during the day, they won't risk it at night. And even if they do, they'll get lost and scattered. No, the Germans will try for the beach or the road."

I saw Grandfather nodding. "I think you are both right, but what bothers me is if the Germans get in the open they'll be able to use mortars and any other heavy weapons they've brought."

He hesitated before adding, "John Henry, Homer, and I all

had experience with rolling barrages during the Great War. I think I speak for them in saying that's an experience we don't want to repeat."

The two old men nodded vigorously.

"Okay, here's the plan. I want these young'uns to drop down the road about a half-mile toward Pigbone. You kids will line up on each side of the road. The rest of us are going to move forward about one hundred yards, to keep them pinned in the house and try to block the road. If they break through us, you young'uns take two shots each. Only two shots! After that, fade into the swamp and head for Pigbone. We will regroup there. And for God's sake, don't shoot each other."

I knew the hole in Grandfather's plan—as I guessed he did too—but I had to ask. "Grandfather, wait," I whispered. "What if they go to the beach?"

"Big Aaron can take care of himself," he said, distracted by his plans.

"But you don't understand. Big Aaron and Willie and Jamie are stretched out opposite the house. Big Aaron put Jigsaw down behind that sand dune to guard the beach—and to keep him safe, I suppose."

"Oh, Lord," he muttered, rolling his eyes heavenward, as if pleading for divine intervention.

Finally, he said in a strong voice, "Harley, do you think you can find Big Aaron in the dark?"

"Yes sir, I think so. I'm willing to try, anyway."

"Okay. You find Big Aaron and tell him what we talked about. Say I suggest he move to a position to block the beach, but make sure he knows it's his decision. He knows his situation better than we do."

I got up to go. I didn't ask for a weapon. I could feel the weight of my father's pistol in my waistband, held securely by my belt.

Beth stood up. "Uncle Perry," she said, "I think I should go with Harley."

"No!"

"Uncle Perry," she whined, "you know Harley's just going to . . ."

I slipped off into the woods, moving as quietly as I could. The sound of Beth's voice followed me into the brush, as she informed Grandfather about my lack of caution and brains. I had lost track of time, but I figured it must be a little after midnight. I had no pocket watch and I had never seen anyone, except in the military and movies, who wore a wristwatch. There may have been six hours until first light, or thirty minutes—I simply had no clue.

Woods at night are full of dangers. I slipped and fell a couple of times until I learned to look for different shades of black. The trees seemed to suck out what scant light existed in the forest, but the puddles found enough light, even on a night as black as the Devil's heart, to produce a dull shimmer. A steady mist dripped from clouds that seemed to hang among the treetops.

Just above the horizon, a red moon seemed to play peek-a-boo among the storm clouds. The words of an old spiritual came back to me. "Oh, when the moon turns red as blood." I tried to block the ancient legend of the blood moon—that it signaled the death of someone close to you—from my mind. I concentrated on the dark woods and tried to block out thoughts of Grandfather and Beth.

Judging distances proved to be impossible in that lightless netherworld. I simply hugged the edge of the road, staying just inside the woods, to keep from getting shot. I would eventually stumble over Big Aaron—I hoped.

"Harley," said a jovial voice from the brush to my left. "You sound like a circus parade—with elephants."

"Is that you, Big Aaron?"

"Last I checked. Harley, what are you doing out here again?"

I quickly explained what had been decided by the war meeting. "Grandfather says the decision is yours."

The decision, however, was made for Big Aaron. Just as I finished my recitation, a single gunshot sounded over by the sand dune. A blast of automatic weapon fire quickly drowned out a second rifle shot and a stream of high-pitched German curses.

Big Aaron and I ran, stumbling and falling in the dark, toward the sand dune. We heard the bushes behind us rattling, and Willie and Jamie emerged from the woods at a dead run, hurrying toward the sound of battle. One of the men yelled, "We're coming, Jigsaw!"

A few pinpricks of light flashed atop the distant sand hill, followed by that angry bee buzz sound of bullets passing just overhead. We all hit the ground and returned fire. I snapped off two quick rounds from the little pistol, and then felt ashamed. At a distance of two football fields, in the dark, and with a .32 caliber pistol, I stood a better chance of throwing a snowball to the moon than I did of hitting anything I shot at. I looked around, embarrassed, but no one seemed to notice.

We began our advance again, but more cautiously now. Big Aaron and I crouched as we ran, stopping frequently to take cover behind rotting boats and barrels, small mounds of sand, or anything else that offered a little protection.

The sand hill, silent and sinister, loomed before us, and we stopped at its base to catch our breath. Both of us were panting, and my sweat-soaked shirt clung to my skinny frame. Big Aaron, though only three or four feet away, was nothing but a shadowy blur.

He leaned close and whispered, "Are you comin' with me, Harley?"

"Yeah."

"Okay, on my signal."

I waited, tense and ready. I did not think about what waited beyond the crest of the dune, Grandfather, or Beth. "You must be the first one over the hill," my frenzied mind repeated over and over.

"Now," came the shout, and we sprang forward.

With his longer, stronger legs, Big Aaron cleared the hill first, with me right at his heels. A single flash of light pierced the darkness, followed by the crack of a rifle. Something slammed into my forehead, scalding like a blow from a red-hot poker.

My knees collapsed, and I tumbled face forward into the sand and lay still. I heard a brief burst of ragged gunfire, followed by silence. I wondered if I had died. I tried to move my legs and they worked fine, so I figured I would live.

I heard Big Aaron's keening wail and thought for a moment that he must have been hit by the same shot that got me. I could only see through one eye. Blood and caked sand had temporarily blinded my left eye, but I saw the large man gently cradling the lifeless body of the moon-faced boy in his arms. He gently ran his free hand over the teen's head, tenderly stroking Jigsaw's hair like a small, favorite kitten.

"Oh, Lord! Oh, Lord! What will I tell your mother?" he asked, as if expecting the dead boy to somehow provide an answer.

I lay still and waited. My head throbbed. The flood of adrenalin that had carried me through the afternoon and the battle ebbed, and weariness and a terrible pain took its place.

Willie and Jamie moved like shadows all over the field. I heard a few scattered gunshots but I lacked the strength to go find out why the men were shooting. Jamie soon reappeared and checked to see if I needed help. Finding that I would likely live, he moved over to comfort Big Aaron.

Grandfather, Beth, and the other men and boys materialized through the rain and fog, moving as silently as specters. Grandfather looked terrible—a limping scarecrow with face contorted with pain and worry—and he leaned at times on Beth for support.

Willie and Jamie came forward to greet the reinforcements and report on the situation.

"Perry," Willie said matter-of-factly, "we think that five of them Germans made their escape in a rubber boat. We could barely see them way out toward the channel. Jamie and me snapped off a couple of shots but didn't come close to hitting anything."

Jamie took up the narrative. "Looks like poor old Jigsaw got off a couple of shots. We found one German gut shot. The other Germans must have figured the wounded man would die and left him there to hold us up while they made their escape. He got off the one shot that got Harley."

"Got Harley?" he screamed. "What do you mean, got Harley?"

"The boy's up on the top of the sand dune—wounded."

The old man bounded up the hill and stopped a few feet from me. From the look on his face, I must have looked awful. He finally sank down beside me and took me in his arms. Grandfather looked so different, cradling me. "Death's first-born," they called him behind his back, but he seemed now only a frail and scared old man.

"I'm so sorry, Harley," he muttered. "I am so sorry. I never meant for you to be in any danger."

"I'm okay, Grandfather," I said, trying to be brave. In fact, I hurt so badly I felt like death warmed over.

Beth had followed the old man. She began wiping my face with a wet rag she found somewhere, gently washing away the blood and sand while the old man held me. When she finished, Beth poured some liquid on the wound that stung like fire.

"You almost scratched my face off last night," I moaned. "Now you're trying to burn off the rest of it."

"Oh hush, you big baby. Half the men here are hurt worse than you, and you are the only one complaining."

When she had done all she could, she found some gauze from somewhere and wrapped it around my head like a turban.

Trucks and horses soon appeared, and Grandfather asked Willie and Jamie to stay behind and guard Ortiz Point. Big Aaron tenderly carried Jigsaw to the back of a truck and laid him on his back. Grandfather told Beth and me that we would ride back there beside the corpse, and we crawled into the bed of the pickup truck.

I started to protest that Grandfather needed to ride with us, but he and Big Aaron climbed in the next truck to watch over the man in the flannel shirt. The prisoner rattled off a few sentences in German, and my grandfather barked back a few words in that foreign tongue and then kicked the commando in the ribs.

"What'd he say?" Big Aaron asked.

"Oh, a bunch of that German garbage about black people. I told him that if he said another word about my friends, I'd tie a rope around his neck and make him run all the way back to Pigbone behind the truck."

The men all laughed a little, except Big Aaron. He was looking at Jigsaw's body and his face was grim.

Two of the black youths went to the front of the trucks and turned the cranks to start the engines, and the odd caravan of horses and vehicles clattered off through the piney woods toward Pigbone.

11

Help of the Helpless

Somehow, the townspeople of Pigbone knew we were coming. Men and women, boys and girls lined the dirt streets, waving a few tiny American flags and cheering the returning warriors. A comic artist would have had great sport painting our odd cavalcade of bloody, weary men (and a boy and a girl) hanging onto twenty-year-old trucks and jaded horses.

Even news of Jigsaw's death failed to entirely dampen the celebration. Their men had fought with the fabled Perry Lang Wallace—Death's firstborn—and stood toe to toe against an army of invaders. The black community believed that the Germans had come to burn Pigbone. Grandfather and I never contradicted that story. That fiction was easier to understand than a conspiracy involving a dusty village on the coast of Africa and a secret airbase.

Black arms hugged me tightly in gentle bear hugs and wet kisses covered my face. Beth seemed to be a special hero of the teenage girls, and they soon formed a phalanx around her as formidable as any Roman Legion. Grandfather received a few handshakes from some of the older black men he knew, but in general they held him in awe.

Big Aaron immediately took charge of the situation. He got

Beth a room at his mother's house. "She sometimes lets rooms to travelers," he explained, "but only if they meet her standards."

I could have told the old lady a thing or two about Beth's temper, but I decided to keep quiet. Otherwise, they might stick her with us, and she'd be bossing us around within a few minutes. A young minister offered Grandfather and me the use of a deserted caretaker's cabin on the church property.

The German prisoner barely escaped being torn limb from limb by the enraged citizens of Pigbone. Only the force of Big Aaron's personality kept the man alive until General Bullard could send troops to take him for interrogation. At first, the German was locked in a root cellar, where he spent his time shouting vulgarities at the black "savages" who passed by—until the owner of the cellar poured a pot of boiling coffee into the pit from an upper window.

After that, Big Aaron posted three teens to keep the man safe. Two of the guards were youngsters who had fought with us at Ortiz Point. I also knew the third watchman. He was the young chicken thief I had seen in the Bullock County Jail. His father had sent him to Pigbone to live with kin and keep him out of trouble. It looked to me that he had made the most of his second chance.

After we stored our gear, Grandfather said, "I guess we ought to go get that old sawbones Pettigrew to sew you up."

I still wore the turban Beth had fashioned at the sand dune. My head ached and not enough aspirin existed in the state of Florida to banish the throbbing.

Dr. Tuskegee hardly fit the stereotype of a kindly, country doctor. The aging physician looked like an old, bald jockey. He had skin the color of light caramel, more wrinkles than a basset hound, and the sourest disposition of any man I'd ever met.

The old quack stitched up the wound on my forehead

without painkillers. "If you were older," he growled, "I'd give you a shot of whiskey. But you young folks always want to show how tough you are. Make you a great scar. It'll really impress the girls."

Most people treated Grandfather with respect, but the way the gnomelike physician poked and prodded the old man you would have thought Grandfather had the habit of paying him with diseased goats.

"Well, Wallace," he grunted as his fingers probed Grandfather's chest, "you are lucky. That rib only missed your lungs by an inch or two. If it hadn't missed, the boy would be negotiating with old Reginald McClure, the undertaker in Lewiston, on the price for his cheapest casket."

Grandfather just looked at him and said, "Well, Pettigrew, I thought they were saving that one for you."

After a few more pleasantries between the equally stubborn and crotchety old codgers, Grandfather went to use the telephone. I knew Grandfather was reporting to General Bullard. The call lasted about a half an hour, and the old man returned more cheerful than he'd been in days. After a little more ill-tempered banter, Grandfather paid our bill and we finally escaped from the grumpy old sawbone's office.

Brother Stumpy arrived in Grandfather's truck in midafternoon. Red rode shotgun, his head hanging out the window and his long ears flapping in the breeze. Brother Stumpy had run into Jamie who told him about the fight and that he could likely find us at Pigbone.

The ladies of Pigbone sent over a feast fit for royalty, and after I stuffed myself I fell asleep almost before my head hit the pillow.

Grandfather shook me awake shortly after noon. "Harley, Harley, wake up," he shouted. "I'm sorry I can't let you sleep longer, but we have to get ready for the funeral."

Someone had washed and ironed my pants and shirt

while I slept, and Grandfather had shined my boots. I could understand wanting to put on our best appearance, but somewhere the old man had found two hideous ties for us. He had already knotted my neckwear, so I slipped it over my head, slid it under my collar, and pulled it tight, wondering again why men had to choke themselves to dress up.

We gathered on a slight hill that overlooked both the town and Lake Seminole. Oaks and tall pines towered over the little cemetery. Many of the mounds had only a name carved on a wooden cross, or burned into a simple plank. Strange configurations of painted rocks and weird carvings of animals marked the sites of a few of the oldest tombs. I wondered if these strange markers had been laid when memories of Africa were still fresh in the minds of the oldest black people.

Jigsaw's family would never have to worry about his tombstone. I don't know how much it cost Grandfather, but he had arranged to have a big headstone lettered, delivered, and set in place in less than a day. It read:

Hiram Elroy Evans
"Jigsaw"
B. 12 July 1926 D. 23 Feb. 1942
He died defending his home and his country.

Grandfather, Brother Stumpy, Beth, and I stood in the back, separated by the color of our skin and lack of knowledge of the deceased. Reverend Alonzo Smith related the sad facts of a life cut too short. He loved and obeyed his momma, he idolized his Uncle Aaron, he attended church, and he loved the simple life of Pigbone. When Jigsaw's mother broke down, sobbing uncontrollably, he took her hand and quoted all of the old scriptures assuring mankind that death was not the end, but the beginning.

Big Aaron spoke with pride of how Jigsaw stood his ground, refusing to run, when those who threatened his hometown came toward him. "He gave his life for you," he said to those assembled. Brother Stumpy led a short prayer and a choir sang hymns of faith and joy.

When I was pretty sure that the service was coming to a close, Grandfather left us, limping slowly to graveside. He looked very old and very tired.

"I am a stranger to many of you. You know who I am, but you do not realize that I am now joined with the good people of Pigbone."

He paused, as if to let the words sink in.

"Reverend Smith asked me to say a few words about Hiram, and I am not much on giving speeches. But Hiram and the people of Pigbone hold a special place in my heart."

I felt sure that Grandfather would end it there, but instead the young minister handed the old man a violin. Grandfather placed the instrument to his chest and played perfectly the slow, haunting hymn, "Abide with Me." Red, hearing his master play, joined in with a low, mournful howling. With the last notes of that bizarre duet still echoing among the trees, Grandfather snapped to attention, raising his hand in salute.

Brother Stumpy put his hand on my shoulder and I noticed I was crying again. When Grandfather came back to where we were standing, we left the graveyard and wandered in silence back to the bungalow.

Grandfather finally spoke. "I have one more duty to the people of Pigbone, and I need to talk to Big Aaron. The ladies here have put together a meal." He turned to me and asked, "You wouldn't mind staying for lunch, would you?"

Brother Stumpy winked at me and said, "I think that is what is known a rhetorical question."

Beth spent the afternoon saying goodbye to her new

friends. Brother Stumpy and Reverend Smith comforted Jigsaw's family, and Grandfather sat with Big Aaron, talking quietly. Being left pretty much alone, I helped myself to some of the finest food I ever put in my mouth.

The sun hung low in the west when Grandfather announced that we had to go.

Brother Stumpy decided that he needed to check the cattle on the southern ranges. He borrowed a horse, took his saddle from the bed of the truck, and disappeared into the piney woods.

Beth went to her sailboat almost as soon as we reached the ranch. "Aunt Rosie must be worried sick," she said.

"I figure that Aunt Rosie has probably been enjoying the first four days of peace she's had in years," I said, figuring a joke would lighten the mood of a goodbye.

"You . . . You stupid boy!" she snapped. She kissed Grandfather's cheek and sailed away without giving me even a backward glance.

Grandfather and I sat on the dock watching the boat disappear. I took off my boots and let my feet dangle into the dark water of the Wildcat. Red soon tired of sitting on the wharf and ran off to check his territory.

"I think you hurt Beth's feelings," the old man finally said quietly.

"Typical girl. She needs to learn to take a joke."

"I reckon you'll probably change your mind about her feelings when you get a little older."

We sat in silence for a long time, watching the sun disappear behind the trees. I stretched out listening to the sounds of the river and the night creatures.

"I want to thank you for saving my life," the old man finally said, his voice little more than a whisper. "I wish your father could have seen your courage at Ortiz Point. He would have been so proud."

A big bass rolled in the shallow water nearby, and bullbats swooped in low over our heads, playing havoc with the mosquitoes. Off in the swamps, far to the south, the unearthly squall of a female panther searching for a mate brought the woodlands to complete silence for a few moments. Even the mindless frogs and insects paid homage to the presence of the ultimate predator with a few seconds of unnatural quiet.

"You know I love you, don't you boy?"

"I figured you did, Grandfather, but it's nice to hear every once in a while."

"You know I'm proud of you?"

After a while the old man said, "We have a lot of work to catch up on tomorrow, and I'm about to fall asleep. We probably ought to head up to the house."

"Yeah, I reckon. It sure is nice to be home," I said. And I meant it.

Epilogue

It is hard to believe that I wrote the account of the firefight at Ortiz Point that you have just read more than sixty years ago. I wish my role had been more heroic, but I did what had to be done.

Grandfather Wallace insisted that I write this history shortly after it happened. He claimed it would help him prepare his report to General Bullard, but I've always suspected he viewed it as an educational project. Whatever his reasoning, it took me more than two months, working at night after a hard day of work, to complete.

Of course, everyone in Timucua County has heard a version of the story. Nothing is ever completely hidden or forgotten in a small town. Local reporters come by about once a year to try to get an exclusive, but I don't like newsmen much. I finally decided to publish this unsanitized account now to correct all the tall tales and outright lies that have sprung up about the so-called Battle of Ortiz Point and so my children and grandchildren will know the true story.

Of course, Grandfather Wallace paid his debt to the people of Pigbone. Sheriff Warren Messer hired Big Aaron Grant as a deputy for the Pigbone area two weeks after Jigsaw's funeral. I don't know how Grandfather pulled this off. In the 1940s, it was political suicide to be seen as a friend of black people, but somehow Perry Lang Wallace browbeat Messer into hiring Big Aaron. At first, the new deputy could only arrest members of his own race, but that changed in time.

Every so often, when we worked the southern cattle ranges, Big Aaron would stop by the campfire to share a cup of coffee and local gossip.

In the 1990s, with the cooling of racial tensions, the citizens of Timucua County, black and white, elected Big Aaron's son as their sheriff. Malcolm Grant was the best law officer the Wildcat Bay area had had since the 1920s—when Perry Lang Wallace served as an interim sheriff.

Simeon Culbertson, one of the teenagers who had fought with us on that night so long ago, joined the Navy. He died when his ship went down in a storm off the Aleutian Islands in 1943. Grandfather and I went to his memorial service.

Brother Stumpy died, in 1949, as he would have wanted. When he missed a Sunday service I went looking for him. He had stopped to rest against an oak tree, where he suffered a massive heart attack. His open Bible lay in his lap.

I finally got my chance to fight in 1950. The politicians called the Korean War a "conflict," a "police action," but it was a war. Ask anyone who fought there.

I fought with the First Marines at the Chosin Reservoir. The battle at the "Frozen Chosin" took place in temperatures reaching minus seventy degrees. I later heard that a writer named Dante said the lowest regions of Hell were icy rather than a nether world of fire and brimstone. He may well be right. I returned home in mid-1951 with three toes amputated due to frostbite and a festering wound from a Chinese bayonet in my side.

Beth and Grandfather met me at Jacksonville and drove me home to Timucua County. The old man looked terrible. He groaned in agony whenever the car hit a pothole and lay on the backseat breathing deeply through most of the trip.

"He's dying," Beth muttered, when we stopped for gas and burgers at Pentecost. "The cancer is eating him alive."

Beth stayed at the ranch, now nursing two invalids. She and I went on long rides together, talking and laughing, until I could no longer deny my love for her. I asked her to marry me at the spring-fed pond where I had nearly killed her so many years before.

Somehow, Grandfather clung to life until after Beth and I were married. He served as my best man, and I could have asked for no better. Norman gave Beth away, crying like a child.

During the fall of 1952, Beth and I buried Grandfather beside Grandmother on the hill overlooking the Wildcat. The newspaper claimed it was the largest funeral in the history of Timucua County. The reporter took note of a large contingent of African-Americans from Pigbone among the mourners.

After the crowd had finally gone, Beth and I stood on the hill by the grave watching the sunset.

"He kept his promise," I said.

"He always did," she said. "But which promise do you mean?"

"He told me the first day we met that he would try to be a good father to me. I think he did a pretty good job."

A breeze from the Gulf rustled the leaves of a nearby oak, and high above the river a red-tailed hawk glided in wide circles on unseen air currents. With tears in our eyes, Beth and I stood hand in hand and watched as the bird disappeared into the sunset.

Historical Notes

African-American soldiers during World War I – The U.S. military continued its long tradition of segregation during World War I, but more than 367,000 black troops enlisted during the Great War. Of those, 100,000 African-Americans served in combat between 1917 and 1918 in France. Major General J. J. Pershing, commander of the American Expeditionary Forces, steadfastly insisted that white U.S. soldiers serve as an independent American army, but he allowed black troops to fight with French divisions, commanded by European officers. One hundred and seventy-one black U.S. soldiers received the French *Croix de Guerre* for "gallantry in action," and Freddie Stowers, an African-American soldier from South Carolina, received the Congressional Medal of Honor.

Blockade runner – During the Civil War, the Union attempted to stop foreign supplies from reaching the Confederacy by blocking any non-U.S. ships from entering Southern ports. Swashbuckling captains, in vessels loaded with European weapons, medicines, and goods unavailable in the South, attempted to slip through the ring of U.S. Navy ships on moonless nights or simply tried to outrun the enemy. Some of these blockade runners were motivated by patriotism to the Confederacy, but others undertook the dangerous business knowing that if they succeeded in reaching a Southern port they could, literally overnight, become fabulously wealthy.

Cattle industry in Florida – Ponce de León brought horses and cattle to Florida in 1521, and a major industry grew from this humble beginning. The state's earliest Spanish and American settlers generally let their cattle range free (unfenced), and early historians noted that the cows became "as wild as deer." The scrawny, long-horned scrub cows flourished on Florida's vast prairies and piney woods, and by 1862 the number of cattle in the state was estimated at 658,000. During the Civil War, Florida's herds became the Confederate army's chief source of food in 1864–1865.

The post-war years were boom times for Florida's cattle industry. The state's cowmen began a lucrative trade with Cuba, exporting cows to the island in exchange for Spanish gold. Early cattle barons, such as Jacob Summerlin and John T. Lesley, drove herds to Gulf ports such as Punta Rassa, Cedar Key, and Tampa, swam the cattle to ships, and transported them by boat to Cuba. Spanish gold became so commonplace that it was said that even the poorest cattleman's child had a rattle made of a tin can containing a couple of gold coins. In the early 1900s, railroads pushed into cattle country, opening trade in Florida beef to the northern and western states.

Many historians believe that "Cracker," the nickname for early white settlers of Florida, is a relic of the state's cattle industry. The name apparently derived from the sound of the ten- to twelve-foot leather whips the cowmen cracked in the air as they herded cattle.

A valuable resource for anyone interested in researching Florida's cattle industry is Joe Akerman's book, *Florida Cowman: A History of Florida Cattle Ranching*.

Florida panthers – Barely fifty of the beautiful, endangered Florida panthers—called mountain lion, cougar, and puma in the Western U.S.—still roam the wildest areas of

South Florida, but until the 1950s they inhabited many undeveloped areas in the state. As late as 1960, the author heard the blood-curdling squall of a female panther calling for a mate along the Marion–Levy County line. Crackers generally referred to these magnificent creatures as "painters."

Cedar Key – The town of Cedar Key was established in the early 1840s, but the island had a long prior history as a way station for the Spanish treasure fleet, pirate haven, and site of a Seminole War fort. After the Civil War, lumber, fishing, cattle, and pencil factories transformed the island into a boom town. Cedar Key's population soared to more than 10,000 residents, but a hurricane destroyed the town in 1896. Cedar Key was rebuilt, the sawmills and pencil factories reopened, but the town never regained its previous prosperity. Cedar Key is today, with fewer than 800 residents, a popular tourist destination.

DSC - Acronym for "Distinguished Service Cross." The DSC is a military award given for "extraordinary heroism" in combat against a foreign enemy.

Dogtrot cabins – The typical settler's home in early Florida often consisted of two square log rooms connected by an open hallway, or dogtrot. As the settlers prospered, they added rooms, porches, and sometimes a second story. The kitchen usually was separated from the house due to the danger of fires. Ronald W. Haase's *Classic Cracker*, published by Pineapple Press, provides an excellent introduction to the evolution of the dogtrot cabins.

Folk burial customs – Early nineteenth-century graveyards holding African-American remains often contain burial mounds paved with shells, rocks, colorful tiles, broken glass, and wooden markers shaped like human heads and shoulders. These unusual burial practices are thought by some anthropologists to be a merger of the "pagan" and Christian beliefs of slaves. Shells, for example, seem to represent "the deceased's passage to the spirit world," while including tile and glass owned by the dead is a form of ancestor worship. See an article by Sherrie Stokes, "Gone but Not Forgotten: Wakulla County's Folk Graveyards," *Florida Historical Quarterly* (October 1991) for additional information.

German U-boat activity in the Gulf – When the United States entered World War II, the German High Command ordered German submarines (called U-boats) into the Gulf of Mexico to stop the vital flow of oil and war materials from ports in Texas and Louisiana. The first German U-boats entered the Gulf by February 1942, and by May, old-timers along the Gulf coast were joking that "there were so many German U-boats in the Gulf, it was a wonder they didn't torpedo each other." U.S. forces were slow in protecting Gulf shipping, and during 1942–1943 the German subs sank at least fifty-six Allied ships in the Gulf.

Lang, David – David Lang served as colonel of the 8th Florida Regiment during the Civil War. Lang was the heart and soul of the Florida troops in General Robert E. Lee's Virginia army. He led the Floridians at Gettysburg, Cold Harbor, and Appomattox—their time of greatest sacrifice, triumph, and defeat. Post-war, Lang remained an "Unreconstructed Rebel." He served on the staff of several governors, including E. A. Perry. Fearing that Prohibitionists might gain power, during the last years of his life he reportedly buried kegs of whiskey throughout the Florida panhandle.

Leathernecks – A nickname for the U.S. Marines, derived from the leather collars the early Marines wore to protect their necks from sword strokes.

Lend-Lease Program – During the 1930s the U.S.

Congress had passed a series of Neutrality Laws designed to keep America out of Europe's wars. By 1940, with Europe and Asia once more embroiled in conflict and England teetering on the brink of defeat, President Franklin D. Roosevelt pushed the Lend-Lease program through the Congress. This allowed FDR to supply the Allies with ammunition, tanks, trucks, food, and airplanes beginning in June 1940. A significant portion of the aid was funneled through Florida along the Takoradi air route. Allied payment for the war material came in the form of leases to the United States for military bases in the Western Hemisphere and a promise of repayment at a later date. America provided a total of forty-nine billion dollars in Lend-Lease aid during World War II.

Citizens and politicians who wanted to keep America out of the war in Europe and Asia harshly criticized President Roosevelt for the Lend-Lease Program.

Mullet – The lowly mullet is a fish rarely found on the menus of fancy restaurants, but it was the seafood of choice for many poor Floridians.

Mullet travel in huge schools in the coastal waters of Florida and the southeastern United States. These game fish can live in salt, brackish, or fresh water, and they feed on tiny plants and organisms on the bottom of shallow bays and creeks. There are over one hundred varieties of mullet, but the most common in west Florida are the silver and black mullet. Barracuda and tarpon trail the mullet migrations, gorging on the fish.

Early residents of Florida would spread dragnets across channels frequently used by the fish and catch hundreds of mullet in a single night. The mullet were cleaned, filleted, and preserved in large barrels of salt in the days before refrigeration.

Perry, Edward A. – This Confederate general from Florida was born in Massachusetts and educated at Yale University. He was practicing law in Pensacola when the Civil War began, and Perry cast his lot with the South. Wounded several times in battle, a severe bullet wound at the Battle of the Wilderness ended his role as a combat leader. Post-war, he returned to his law practice and was elected governor of Florida in 1884.

Radios – Radios used during the 1940s usually contained both AM and short-wave bands. Transmitters, receivers, or a combination (called transceivers) were also common in many U.S. homes. President Franklin D. Roosevelt used the nation's airwaves to communicate with ordinary Americans in his famous fireside chats, and country music attained popularity due to radio. Only a very few automobiles had car radios. Where electricity was not available, large batteries served as the power source.

Screwworms – Florida ranchers blamed the importation of "Dust Bowl" cattle from Oklahoma and Texas for the introduction of screwworms to the Sunshine State. The female screwworm laid its eggs in an animal's open wound, and when the eggs hatched they could eat a cow alive in three days. Ranchers had to quit branding, ear cutting, and using whips and cow dogs, which might create a cut or opening in the animal's hide. A University of Florida scientist ended the epidemic by flooding the state with sterile (not producing offspring) female screwworms in 1959. (See Akerman, *Florida Cowman*).

Swabbies – A derogatory nickname for U.S. Navy sailors, derived from the common activity of swabbing, or mopping, the decks of their ships.

Takoradi air route – Before the U.S. entered World War II in December 1941, German U-boats and the German Air Force (Luftwaffe) seriously damaged Allied shipping of Lend-Lease war materials to Great Britain and the Soviet Union in the North Atlantic. To get around this problem, the Army Air Corps and Lend-Lease authorities developed a plan to ferry aircraft across the South Atlantic. This became known as the Takoradi air route.

Planes built by American aircraft factories were flown to Florida, then through the Antilles, and on to Brazil. American pilots flew the planes across the narrows of the South Atlantic to Takoradi where they were turned over to the Royal Air Force (RAF).

This route became largely unnecessary when the United States entered the war. Allied planners developed a method using large convoys of ships to cross the Atlantic to England, which neutralized the U-boat wolf packs.

Unfortunately, few sources have been found regarding the role Florida played in this important part of America's war effort.

Texas tick fever – Texas tick fever had been a problem in the West for many years, but it appeared in Florida's cattle range just before World War I. The tick fever attacked the red blood cells of the cows and deer it infected, causing a slow, agonizing death for the unfortunate animal. Fencing the cattle ranges and periodic dipping of cattle in an arsenic solution finally eliminated this disease.

Tommies – Nickname for British soldiers.

Wake Island – On December 8, 1941, a huge Japanese invasion force assaulted 450 Marines on Wake Island commanded by Major James P. S. Devereux. For sixteen days the outnumbered, outgunned Marine, Navy, and native fighters stubbornly fought off repeated Japanese attacks. The

Allied press labeled Wake Island "the Alamo of the Pacific," and like the brave Texas defenders, the doomed American troops raised the spirits and bought time for a nation still reeling from the raid on Pearl Harbor. The Marines sank two Japanese destroyers, shot down seven enemy airplanes, and inflicted over one thousand casualties before surrendering.

World War I – President Woodrow Wilson was reelected in 1916 using the slogan "He kept us out of war," and many Americans truly wanted to stay neutral. That attitude began to change when a German submarine sank the *Lusitania*, a British cruise ship carrying American citizens (and probably ammunition for the British army). When the Zimmermann Telegraph (whereby Germany tried to persuade Mexico to invade the American Southwest) became public, Wilson felt compelled to ask for a declaration of war.

By then the war had been raging in Europe and Africa for three years. Trenches stretched across Western Europe, and hundreds of thousands of men would die to take a single mile of enemy territory. Both the Central Powers (Germany, Austria-Hungary, and the Turkish Ottoman Empire) and the Allies (Great Britain, France, the U.S., and Russia) used airplanes, machine guns, tanks, and poison gas extensively, making World War I the first modern conflict.

Doughboys, the nickname for American soldiers and Marines, began arriving France in June 1917, and they could not have arrived at a better time. Several French regiments were in a state of mutiny. The Russian Czar had been killed by Bolshevik revolutionaries who immediately made peace with Germany, thereby releasing hundreds of thousands of German troops for use against the French and English.

The Doughboys pumped fresh blood and enthusiasm into the Allied cause. After a few months of training, they became ferocious fighters. In July and August 1918 the Americans helped halt a German offensive designed to take Paris and end the war. The Americans counterattacked, driving the enemy back to the Seigfried Line (the German border). The Germans signed an Armistice, and World War I ended on November 11, 1918.

In less than a year of fighting, the 320,710 Americans were killed or wounded.

World War II – The Japanese bombing of the U.S. Pacific fleet at Pearl Harbor, on December 7, 1941, catapulted America into World War II. As in World War I, Europeans and Asians had been fighting for some time before the United States entered the conflict. America's major allies were Great Britain, the Soviet Union, and China. Opposing the Allies were Germany, Italy, and Japan, known as the Axis powers.

Forces of the German Fuhrer (Leader) Adolph Hitler had swept through Europe using planes and tanks in a rapid style of attack known as a "Blitzkrieg" (lightning war). They quickly captured Poland, France, and much of North Africa. Only England and Russia continued to fight back. Hitler's forces attempted to batter the British to their knees in a furious air attack, while simultaneously invading the Soviet Union.

Meanwhile, Japanese troops experienced similar early successes. They captured large portions of China, Burma, and a huge English army at Singapore. Soon after the Pearl Harbor attack, the Japanese captured a large American army in the Philippines, and people along the U.S. West Coast lived in fear of a Japanese invasion of America.

By 1943, the U.S. and her allies began the slow process of taking back the territory lost to the Axis. At Guadalcanal (August 1942–February 1943) the Marines won a hard-fought victory and began a bloody campaign of "island-hopping" toward the Japanese homeland. In the west, successes in North Africa and the invasion of Italy paved the way for D-Day and the liberation of France.

The human cost of World War II was staggering by any measure. It has been estimated that sixty million people died as a result of the conflict, including millions of Jews slaughtered in Hitler's Holocaust. The U.S. had sixteen million troops at arms during World War II. The American military suffered more than 300,000 battle deaths, and more than one million total casualties.

If you enjoyed reading this book, here are some other fiction titles from Pineapple Press. To request a catalog or to place an order, write to Pineapple Press, P.O. Box 3889, Sarasota, Florida 34230, or call 1-800-PINEAPL (746-3275). Or visit our website at www.pineapplepress.com.

Escape to the Everglades by Edwina Raffa and Annelle Rigsby. Based on historical fact, this young adult novel tells the story of Will Cypress, a half-Seminole boy living among his mother's people during the Second Seminole War. He meets Chief Osceola and travels with him to St. Augustine. (hb)

Escape to the Everglades Teacher's Activity Guide by Edwina Raffa and Annelle Rigsby. The authors of *Escape to the Everglades* have written a teacher's manual filled with activities to help students learn more about Florida and the Seminoles. Includes references to the Sunshine State Standards. (pb)

Solomon by Marilyn Bishop Shaw. Young Solomon Freeman, and his parents, Moses and Lela, survive the Civil War, gain their freedom, and gamble their dreams, risking their very existence, on a homestead in the remote environs of north central Florida. (hb)

A Land Remembered: Student Edition by Patrick D. Smith. This well-loved, best-selling novel tells the story of three generations of the MacIveys, a Florida family battling the hardships of the frontier, and how they rise from a dirt-poor cracker life to the wealth and standing of real estate tycoons. Now available to young readers in two volumes. (hb & pb)

Middle School Teacher Plans and Resources for A Land Remembered: Student Edition by Margaret Paschal. The vocabulary lists, comprehension questions, and post-reading activities for each chapter in *A Land Remembered: Student Edition* make this teacher's manual a valuable resource. The activities aid in teaching social studies, science, and language arts coordinated with the Sunshine State Standards. (pb)

The Spy Who Came In from the Sea by Peggy Nolan. In 1943 fourteen-year-old Frank Holleran sees an enemy spy land on Jacksonville Beach. First Frank needs to get people to believe him, and then he needs to stop the spy from carrying out his dangerous plans. Winner of the Sunshine State Young Reader's Award. (hb & pb)

Florida's Past by Gene Burnett. Collected essays from Burnett's "Florida's Past" columns in *Florida Trend* magazine, plus some original writings not found elsewhere. Burnett's easygoing style and his sometimes surprising choice of topics make history good reading. **Volume 1** (pb); **Volume 2** (pb); **Volume 3** (pb)

CRACKER WESTERNS

Bridger's Run by Jon Wilson. Tom Bridger has come to Florida in 1885 to find his long-lost uncle and a hidden treasure. It all comes down to a boxing match between Tom and the Key West Slasher. (hb & pb)

Ghosts of the Green Swamp by Lee Gramling. Saddle up your easy chair and kick back for a Cracker Western featuring that rough-and-ready but soft-hearted Florida cowboy, Tate Barkley, introduced in *Riders of the Suwannee.* (hb)

Guns of the Palmetto Plains by Rick Tonyan. As the Civil War explodes over Florida, Tree Hooker dodges Union soldiers and Florida outlaws to drive cattle to feed the starving Confederacy. (hb & pb)

Ninety-Mile Prairie by Lee Gramling. While Peek Tillman herds cattle to market in late nineteenth–century Florida, he's on the lookout for wild beasts and poisonous reptiles—as well as predators of the human variety. He gets more than he bargained for when he sets out to rescue a Yankee archaeologist and his beautiful wife from what he believes is a doomed expedition. (hb & pb)

Riders of the Suwannee by Lee Gramling. Tate Barkley returns to 1870s' Florida just in time to come to the aid of a young widow and her children as they fight to save their homestead from outlaws. (hb)

Thunder on the St. Johns by Lee Gramling. Riverboat gambler Chance Ramsay teams up with the family of young Josh Carpenter and the trapper's daughter Abby Macklin to combat a slew of greedy outlaws seeking to destroy the dreams of honest homesteaders. (hb & pb)

Trail from St. Augustine by Lee Gramling. A young trapper, a crusty ex-sailor, and an indentured servant girl fleeing a cruel master join forces to cross the Florida wilderness in search of buried treasure and a new life. (hb)